RUN FOR COVER

by John Welcome

"Humour and the kind of romance that is associated with dry martini and sun-glasses rather than with moonlight and apple-blossom, make the tale an agreeable one." —*Times Literary Supplement*

"Sophisticated, sexy . . . it goes at a lick." —*Spectator*

"An escape number of considerable liveliness." —*San Francisco Chronicle*

"Has real speed." —*Saturday Review*

RUN FOR COVER

by

John Welcome

PERENNIAL LIBRARY
Harper & Row, Publishers
New York, Cambridge, Philadelphia, San Francisco
London, Mexico City, São Paulo, Sydney

AUTHOR'S NOTE

There is no such village as Ste Marguerite and I have
taken some small liberties with the geography of the
Coast in imagining its position. I am sure, however,
that anyone familiar with the Gulf of St Tropez will
have no difficulty in visualizing the position which I
have dreamed up for it. In the meantime it remains
wholly fictitious as do the characters herein portrayed.
None of them—not even the narrator—bears any re-
semblance to any living person.

J.W.

A hardcover edition of this book was published in 1958 by Faber &
Faber Ltd, London, England. It is here reprinted by arrangement
with Sterling Lord Agency.

First PERENNIAL LIBRARY edition published 1983.

LIBRARY OF CONGRESS CATALOG CARD NUMBER: 83-47589

ISBN: 0-06-080664-8

83 84 85 86 87 10 9 8 7 6 5 4 3 2 1

One

A TYPESCRIPT FROM THE TOMB

It was quite by chance that I caught the early train from Tonbridge that morning. I had been spending the week-end with George Verschoyle. He had intended to go to London for the day so I said that I would go up on the same train. Then something happened, a horse got cast in his box, I think, and there was trouble in the yard so what with one thing and another he put off his trip. However, I thought I was as well out of the way so I stuck to my original idea of getting the early train. George's wife drove me to the station and we cut it pretty fine. I had just time to pull open a carriage door and to jump in as the train was starting. I put my bag on the rack and when I sat down I found myself facing a man I knew quite well.

His name was Robin Saunders and he was the senior partner in the publishing firm of Saunders and Renton. He was a member of my club and I sometimes lunched with him or had a drink with him in the evenings. He had originally been with another firm, one of the old-established ones who thought a lot of themselves and the "prestige of their imprint" as they described it in their advertisements and correspondence. The firm had refused to take him into partnership so he had set up on his own alone with Renton who ran the business end of it and whom I didn't know. They had got substantial backing from somewhere, and they had done very well. Several of the older firm's authors had come away with Saunders and he had, I think, whatever peculiar flair or nose for a book or call it what you like which makes the successful publisher.

He was a great believer in getting outside opinions on manuscripts submitted to him. To take a very simple instance—if he had a book about the R.A.F. which he was thinking about accepting he would get someone who knew about flying to read it, not so much for authenticity, though that came into it too, but for what he called, in a word of his own, "the zing". This I can only roughly translate as the general impact which the book made upon an expert in its own sphere. "I can do the literary end of it myself," he would say. "I want to find out the effect it has on the unliterary chap. I want to know if it's *right*." He was passionately interested in his job as any successful publisher must be, and this was one of his hobby horses. "The ordinary man", he would say, "can tell you when he's losing interest. He doesn't know anything about technique but I do. I can tell why and where the ordinary man ought to lose interest. If both opinions coincide then the book is out."

I used to chaff him about all this, telling him that

publishing books was as inexact a science as backing horses and that the system he used was just as fallible as any other system of picking winners. But he had employed me quite often as a working part of this system and by and large I had been pretty useful to him. I had good qualifications as a guinea-pig. I had been a prisoner of war for the best part of a year having been picked up during a raid on the French coast. Then I had escaped and got out through Spain. I had been able to advise him on the P.O.W. and escape stuff which had started to pour into every publisher's office a few years after the war. When I had returned to England I had been put on hush-hush work which I wasn't supposed even yet to talk about. They had been a pretty rum bunch in that outfit—misfits, drunks, cranks and queers, all of them useful in one capacity or another; many of them, in my opinion, only wanting a push, or perhaps a twist would be a better word, to go from being with us to being against us. Some of these gentry had written their memoirs after the war and one or two of the typescripts had come into Saunders's office. Here, too, without saying much, I had been able to help him and to steer him out of trouble with the official secrets' people and consequent loss of money if they were to clamp down on a book already set up in print. Then, in another sphere, my racing associations were a help, so that altogether Saunders regarded me, I think, as something of a bright boy.

We chatted idly going up in the train about such

diverse subjects, I remember, as the Test matches, the Anglo-American Conference due to open soon in Paris and the Abominable Snowman. But Saunders could never keep away from shop for long. He told me two publishing stories, highly defamatory, about the present conduct of his old firm, omitting, however, to tell me, which I knew, that he himself had turned down the current Book Society fiction choice and that they had taken it. I mentioned this gently to him but he was never one to admit to a mistake. "I wish them the very greatest of luck with it," he said. "Poor things, I hear they need it."

Suddenly he reached up and pulled down his brief-case from the rack. "I've got something here right up your street," he said. "Cloak and dagger stuff. Needs working on, but I think there may be a book in it."

The train was pulling alongside the platform. He stood up, took down his umbrella and bowler, put the half-opened brief-case under his arm and stepped out. I followed him. "Read it for me," he said, as we walked along. "I want to know if it's bogus. Let me have a report as soon as you can, there's a good chap." He pushed the typescript into my hand. "It is by someone I never heard of. Name of Rupert Rawle."

I stopped dead in my tracks.

"Rupert!" I exclaimed. "Rupert Rawle! But he's dead!"

But Saunders had gone, swallowed up in the hurrying throng.

I stood like a fool staring at the typescript. There it was in block capitals on a white label pasted to the front cover: WATERS OF STRIFE BY RUPERT RAWLE. But Rupert was dead. I knew he was. He had died five years ago when he drove his Jaguar over the cliff between Lavandou and St. Clair. His broken car and his broken body had been picked up the next morning. There was no doubt about that—or was there? I put the typescript under my arm and made my way through the barrier.

I have a small top flat in Knightsbridge, behind Harrods. I am not much there and it suits me well enough. The first thing I did when I got in was to ring up Saunders. His secretary told me he was at a manuscript meeting and would not be free until the afternoon. I put the telephone down and picked up the typescript.

There was no address on the fly-leaf. It merely repeated the title and the name of the author. I weighed the book in my hand, wondering what was in it. I wanted to read it yet I dreaded doing so. Rupert and I had had our lives too closely intertwined at one period for me to look forward with any pleasure to reading his book, if, indeed it was his book. I had been, I supposed, his best friend; I had all but worshipped him with the silly, callow, subaltern's worship of a glamorous superior officer. Then I had feared and distrusted him. Finally I had hated him. These stages were progressive. I had a six-inch scar on my right thigh incurred on that raid when I was captured to mark the time of my fear and distrust. I had a scar somewhere deep inside me to mark the time of my hatred. I could still remember the letter I had received when I was a prisoner of war. It was that letter which had made me take the fantastic chance of escaping in the way I did, and perhaps it was the way fate recompenses you for bad luck which had allowed me to get away with it. Jacquie—was there anything about her in the book, I wondered. I had done my best to forget her. After Rupert's death I had made no effort to find her. I told myself that that chapter in my life had been closed for ever. And I didn't want to reopen it now.

Yet I knew that I had to read the book. But not just now, I thought. I was not going to rush at it. I had made appointments to see my stockbroker and the accountants who do my income-tax. I would keep these, have lunch at my club, come back in the afternoon and read the book through at my leisure.

I picked up my papers and glanced through them. I take *Sporting Life*, *The Daily World* and *The Times*, and I read them in that order. Today I was in something of a hurry so I put *Sporting Life* aside until the afternoon and glanced at the headlines in *The Daily World*. An American senator had been letting fly at British policy in the Middle East and Britain generally, and there were banner headlines of his speech. There was nobody I knew either dead or engaged according to *The Times*. I read the racing column and the cricket scores and then turned to the leader. "Stresses and Strains" this was headed. It concerned Anglo-American relations and took as its text the same senator's speech which was annoying *The Daily World*. It expressed the opinion at some length that allies must give and take and pull together. On the leader page, too, was an indignant letter on the subject of our being ruled from Washington. This letter had pride of place at the top of the column and was signed by a well-known hard-hitting peer. Someone, it seemed, was rocking the boat.

I went into my bedroom and changed out of my tweeds. As I was letting myself out I saw the typescript lying where I had left it on a side table. I couldn't help myself; I picked it up and began to leaf through it. The very first sentence caught my eye: "They make excellent champagne cocktails in Klèber's in the Rue Royale." Well, that was typical of Rupert, anyway, I thought. He liked champagne cocktails as he liked most of the good things of life, and he didn't care who paid for them as long as it wasn't himself. The little clock on my mantelpiece struck eleven. Realizing that I should never get my business done unless I hurried, I put down the typescript and went out.

It was close on three o'clock when I returned to the flat. I had had a couple of glasses of port with my lunch and I felt pleasantly drowsy and anaesthetized and ready to face Rupert's book. I hung up my hat and umbrella, came into the living-room and turned to the side-table where I had left the typescript.

The book was gone.

I stood quite still for a moment as the surprise of the thing hit me and then my mind began to react as it had been taught to do. No one had a key to the flat except myself. I examined the Yale lock on the front door. It had not been tampered with. Systematically I went through the entire contents of the flat. Nothing else had been touched. Whoever had done this had come for no other purpose than to take the typescript.

I sat down and began to consider my position. In the first place I had lost a publisher's typescript. This, in the end, was likely to be the least of my problems, but it was the most immediate one. I wondered where Saunders had got the book from. I pulled the telephone towards me. This time Saunders was available.

"Got it from an agent," he replied. "Someone I'd never heard of before. Must have just set up. An address in Crutched Friars of all places. Hang on a moment, as it happens I've got the file on my desk. Here you are. Scruffy postcard clipped on to the cover of the typescript. James A. Wells, 119 Close Court, Crutched Friars. What is it about this book? Someone else has been ringing up all the morning. Wouldn't take no for an answer. Hauled me out of a manuscript meeting."

I felt my pulses start to race. "Someone else?" I said, as calmly as I could. "Can you tell me who it was?"

"The author as a matter of fact."

"What!" I shouted. "But he can't. He's dead."

"Is he, by Gad! Speaks very clearly for a disembodied spirit. Writes well, too. I must prescribe it for some of my other authors. What is all this?"

"It may be more important than you think. What did he want?"

"He wanted the book. I told him it had gone to an outside reader. He was most pressing. Said he had to have it back for alteration. In the end I gave him your name. Silly of me, I suppose. Nice for you to meet him again, though. Or his ghost. I've always wondered how Hamlet felt. Now you can tell me. You'd better give it to him if he identifies himself."

"You needn't worry," I said. "He's got it. The book has gone."

"What!"

"Yes. It's a fact. It's been stolen somehow. I'm not quite sure how yet."

There was a pause and then Saunders spoke again. "Do you want to see me about this?" he asked.

"Yes," I answered. "I think perhaps I do."

"Very well, I'll come round." There was a click as he hung up.

I thought for a moment and then I took up the telephone and dialled a number which is not in the book. I wanted two pieces of information and it was important that I asked for them in the right order. I had a feeling that I was going to get choked off about the second one and, as it happened, I was right.

When the call came through I asked for an extension number. After a moment: "Robinson, metal-work department speaking," a voice said. I identified myself and then asked my first question. "Crutched Friars," the voice said. "Repeat the name and address again. Right. I'll get someone on to that right away." I heard a key flip on a desk box and instructions given into it.

I had often wondered what Robinson was like, who he was or where he worked, for I had never seen him. He was to me a disembodied voice high, precise and intelligent, a piece of the vast network with which my life had been closely linked and which I now touched only occasionally and at the edges. "And what else?" the high, carrying voice came clearly down the phone.

I drew my breath. "Look," I said. "Rupert Rawle, he's supposed to be dead, isn't he?"

"Rupert Rawle is dead," the voice answered without hesitation. "Dead," it repeated, "quite dead."

I ploughed on. "What if he isn't?" I said. "Were there any proper check-ups? I think I may have come across something——"

This time the voice cut in on me. This time there was a harsher note in it. "Rawle is dead," it said. "Very dead—and forgotten." The line went blank.

I stared at the phone in my hand for a second or two. Then I put it down. It had been much as I had thought save that I had been smacked down a little more smartly than I had expected. It was all in a piece with what had gone before. Perhaps I had been a fool to open my mouth at all about Rupert—I put these thoughts aside and began to go through the flat again. In my little hall I noticed something which I had missed before. The curtains of the window at the end of the hall were susurrating in a breeze. The window was wide open and I had not left it so. I went along and looked out. Below me was a ledge of ample width for an active man to stand upon. There was only a gap of about five feet between that ledge and the coping of the roof of the next house from which, a few yards away, a fire-escape led down. Too easy, I thought. I closed the window and as I did so my doorbell rang. I went down the hall and admitted Saunders.

"So," the publisher said, as he eased his long body into a chair. "You've lost a manuscript. Very reprehensible. Why, by the way, don't you live somewhere more compatible with your means? All those stairs—I nearly had a heart attack."

"It suits me," I said shortly. "In the winter I'm riding. Summer I'm often abroad. First, from the strictly business point of view how much does it matter losing this?"

"I *never* look at anything from the strictly business point of view. 'While every care is taken no responsibility, etc.,' is our motto. I should think you're all right if that's what is worrying you. But it isn't, is it? If someone has gone to the length of pinching this book to get it back there must be something damn odd about it. What is it? I smell a seller. And I", he added modestly, "can smell one ten miles away. Hence my success."

"What was in the book?" I asked. "I had only time to glance at it. Did you read it?"

He gave me a withering glance. "Of course I read it," he said. "Unlike a certain celebrated literary agent I always read the books I personally handle. It was cloak and dagger stuff. From what I could see excellent of its kind. Well written, too—I never publish a badly written book." Thinking about the book had aroused his excitement. He got up from his chair, tried to prance about the tiny room and failed. Then he stretched out a long forefinger and tapped me on the chest. "But there was more in it than that," he went on. "The fellow had something to say. It wasn't just another cut and thruster. He was putting down what made people do these things—if it can be put down, which I doubt. He was trying, anyway."

"Were you going to publish it?" I asked.

"It needed cutting and cohesion and polishing. He didn't know much about construction, your Mr. Rawle. But yes, if it got the O.K. from you that it wasn't bogus, I'd have taken it."

"Had anyone else read it? Don't you have to get opinions from others in the firm before you finally take a book?"

"If I like a book other opinions are a mere formality.

I decide—I take it." Saunders threw out his arm grandiloquently and smacked his knuckles, hard, against the first racing cup I had ever won, at the Bullingdon Grind years ago. "Dammit," he exclaimed irritably, picking up the cup and reading the inscription. "Why must you live in a mousetrap where I can't move without falling over some relic of a barbarous sport?"

At that moment the telephone rang and I picked it up. "That address in Crutched Friars you inquired about," the voice said. "It's an accommodation address. James A. Wells has cancelled his use of it." The line went dead again.

"Your Mr. Wells, the agent, is no longer at Crutched Friars," I said, as I hung up. "So he wouldn't have got the typescript anyway. If Rupert Rawle wrote that book you can take my word for it that it's authentic. Moreover if he wrote it I've an idea that many people besides ourselves would like to see it, only they wouldn't be reading it for its literary qualities. Can you remember anything that was in it?"

"Very little, dear boy. We've had a lot of them in lately. As for the incidents I can never tell th'other from which. I read a book for the *impact*." Saunders showed every inclination of being about to prance once more. He began to fling out an arm, almost collided with another trophy and arrested the gesture in mid-air.

"Don't knock that down," I said mildly. "I have to

19

return it. It's the Foxrock Cup. I won it in Ireland last March."

"What for—pig-sticking?"

"Let's get back to the point. Can you remember anything about this book at all?"

Saunders sat down. "I wish you wouldn't cross-examine me," he said petulantly. "However, there was a background of Yugoslavia, Paris and the south of France. At least I think that's the one."

"It sounds as if it might be. Can you remember anything else?"

"Just this. The very first sentence was about there being excellent champagne cocktails at a place in the Rue Royale."

"Klébers. I know it. I read the first sentence, too. That's all I read."

"It's not often I get books from dead authors. You've lost the typescript, you know, Graham. I think it is up to you to clear the air for me a bit. That is, if you can. Is Rawle dead?"

"I'm not sure," I said slowly. "I thought he was, but I'm not so sure now. Officially he's dead all right. It appeared in *The Times*—Major the Honourable Rupert Rawle, D.S.O., M.C. and bar. And a chap I know, a journalist in Paris who was in the Resistance and whom we both knew, confirmed it to me. But now, I wonder——"

"Did you know him well?"

"Yes. By and large, I suppose, no one knew him

better. For a long time anyway. And then—then, I don't want to go into this too deeply, I found out something about him. It was something so ghastly", I said slowly, reliving that moment of shock when I opened the letter and its enclosure tumbled out on to my lap, "that I was knocked endways. At first I couldn't believe it. I wanted time to think. And, thinking it over, other little things which I suppose I had noticed almost subconsciously, began to add up. We were doing a raid on the French coast that night and Rupert was leading us. I suppose I should have done something before we went, but my mind was in such a whirl and the ties of old friendship were still so strong that I didn't. I got knocked out on that raid. The Germans picked me up and patched me up. . . ." I paused for a moment staring out over the roof-tops, my mind back in that desperate moment when the Jerries jumped us.

The publisher's voice brought me back to the present.

"Did Rawle get away?" he asked.

"He got away all right," I answered grimly. "I found that much out after I escaped. But I found out precious little else. Someone was covering his tracks. Determined as I was to let nothing stand in the way of my finding him, still I failed. There was a personal reason for my looking for him—something he had done to someone I was very fond of while I was a P.O.W. But there was another reason and a good one. That night on the raid, the person who shot me thought he'd made a job of it. He thought he'd killed me and closed my mouth for ever from asking questions about him. But he hadn't. There was a hell of a flurry going on and for once he bungled what he set out to do. The person who shot me was Rupert Rawle."

Two

CHAMPAGNE COCKTAILS ON THE RUE ROYALE

Saunders's reaction was typical. He stuck out a long, prehensile finger and jabbed me in the chest. "There's a book in this," he said. "And I want it. Do you want a contract?"

"I'll see my solicitor first," I said sourly. "My God, Saunders, I believe you go to bed with a book."

"I've been to bed for one in my time. What are you going to do next?"

"I'm going to find Rupert—if he is alive."

"How do you propose to set about that?"

I drew a deep breath and looked at him and thought. I had already made up my mind what I was going to do, but I was not sure how much of my plans I was going to tell him. Then it occurred to me that it might not be a bad idea if there was one person who knew at least something of where I was going and what I had in mind. Things had a way of happening to one on the sort of jaunt I proposed taking. Saunders for all his eccentricity was, I knew, utterly reliable. It would be no harm to put him in possession of some of the facts. If anything happened to me he could decide for himself whether to follow them up.

"Before the war," I said, "Rupert Rawle was the best G.R. in the country—by a street. He was as good as any of the chaps who were on the top in the golden age of amateur riding—Harry Brown, Tuppy Bennett and Fred Thackray. He headed the amateur list three times —the first when he was only a kid. But for the war he would have been practically a permanency there. He was also a brilliant soldier of the Commando type. He was too unorthodox to have done much good in ordinary service but the Commandos were just cut out for him. They were called Special Companies, if you remember, at the beginning and he was one of the original volunteers. He was something of a swash-buckler and he had the hell of an attractive personality. Women fell for him and men worshipped him. I had admired him from afar when I was a very raw beginner as an amateur rider. When I came to serve with him I fell completely under his spell. He took me up in the way chaps like him sometimes do to a raw and admiring junior. Even after Dunkirk there were still chances to get away to odd race meetings. We were rather encouraged to do it as a matter of fact. I suppose he taught me whatever I know about riding races. He also taught me how to live. He liked the best, did Rupert, and he didn't much care how he got it—the best rides in the best races, the best place when riding a race, the best women and the best drinks. A chap he'd ridden rings around in a race once said to me that racing only came third with Rupert, for he liked women and drink better in that order and that he must have been bloody good at the other two! You may remember the pictures of him in the papers during the war, and the press reports. He was about the first of the army's heroes to be built up in opposition to the glamour boys of the R.A.F. Altogether it was quite a thing when I discovered that he was a traitor. Even then he was too good for me. He knew that I'd guessed or found out somehow. He meant killing me when he shot me in that mêlée, but he just missed out in the end. At least that's how it looks to me. But I was never absolutely certain, never convinced beyond every shadow of a doubt. There was always that last ultimate 'if'. But one thing I do know and that is that when I came back from prison camp I found that he had gone—and taken my girl with him. Now you see why, if he is alive, I want to find him."

"Where do you start?"

"I'm going to tell you this and no more. If anything happens to me you can make what use you like of the information. There is a journalist in Paris called Paul Morel. He was a Free Frenchman and came with us on some of our early raids. Then he went into one of the cloak-and-dagger groups which operated with the Resistance and did very well, I believe. He knew a lot about Rupert and it was to him that I went when I heard that Rupert was dead. He told me then that it was true, that it was Rupert whose body had been picked up, that he was really dead. I think I only believed it then because I wanted to. Morel may well know more than he has said. He has helped me in various ways, currency and such-like, in France since the war. I shall go to Paris tomorrow to see him."

"And then?"

"That depends upon Morel." But I had another idea, too, which I was not divulging yet.

Saunders got up to go. He was unwontedly serious. "I can't say I care much for the sound of Major Rawle," he said. "If he shot you once he may well do so again. Perhaps you'd send me a daily wire from Paris to say that you are all right."

"I'll do that," I said.

He paused for a moment on the landing. "Try and bring that typescript back with you, there's a good chap," he said. "You know that might be quite a book."

I closed the door and took up the telephone.

At five o'clock the following afternoon I met Morel in a restaurant on the Champs-Elysées.

Paul Morel was small, dark and very dapper with a thin pencil line of moustache across his upper lip. He was a conceited, humourless little man and I was never quite sure how far I trusted him.

We shook hands and I sat down. There was a Dubonnet and a packet of Caporal in front of Morel. I had the

26

impression that someone had left him just before my arrival.

"Your wire said that it was urgent," Morel said.

"Yes." Now that I was here I didn't quite know how to start. I drew on the Caporal he had given me, thinking. Then I made up my mind and plunged straight in.

"I do not think that Rupert is dead," I said.

Morel's expression did not change. "And what gives you that opinion, my friend?" he asked.

"Well, I've heard talk——"

"Talk!" Morel's tone was contemptuous. "Talk! They said these things about Lawrence, too. You have not brought me here to discuss the chatter of Mayfair and the race-tracks."

"No, I haven't. I've seen evidence—at least you could call it evidence, I suppose——"

"What sort of evidence?" For the first time in the conversation I thought I heard a quickening of interest in his voice.

I debated what I would say. I didn't want to reveal the existence of the manuscript. "There's a letter written by him," I said.

"Indeed? To whom?"

"To a publisher."

Morel sat up quite straight. He crushed out his cigarette in an ashtray. "That letter is a forgery," he said. "Rupert is dead." He got up to go. As he passed me he laid a hand lightly on my shoulder. "Has he not caused you enough trouble, my friend," he said quietly. "Do not let his shade cause you any more." Then he was gone, an erect little man mingling with the sauntering crowds on the pavement.

I sat on, smoking. The breeze whispered in the trees, all the lovely light of Paris in early summer was about me. I relaxed in it and I thought. I was not in the least impressed with what Morel had said. I believed him to be concealing something, but I might be wrong in this. But I was sure that Rupert was alive and, that being so, I had to find him. The trouble was where to start. Well, there were a couple more coverts for me to draw. If they were blank I could think again. But perhaps they wouldn't be blank.

I called the waiter and paid my score. Then I strolled gently down the way Morel had gone. I crossed the Place de la Concorde, turned into the Rue Royale and walked up it until I came to Kléber's.

It was a sidewalk café and a good one. I knew it well. The embassy staff used it and people from Nato, and it was a great place on a Sunday morning for drinks or coffee after service in the embassy church.

It was the cocktail hour and the place was pretty full, but I found a table at the back. I ordered a champagne cocktail.

Rupert was right, of course, as he always was in matters of this sort. The cocktail was excellent. I sipped it and smoked. Time went along. The cocktail crowd began to thin. I ordered another and went on sipping, surveying my fellow-drinkers. Then suddenly my pulse began to go faster.

Two tables away a young man was sitting. A large pair of smoked glasses covered most of the upper portion of his face so that I could not be sure of the direction of his glance. I thought, however, that he was looking at me and had been doing so for some little time. He was drinking a champagne cocktail.

I stared back at him or at as much of him as those huge smoked glasses would admit. Without moving my eyes I raised my glass.

With a sudden smooth movement, rather like a cat, he got to his feet, pushed back his chair and took up his glass. The next instant he was standing beside me.

"They make excellent champagne cocktails here," he said. He was wearing a double-breasted blue blazer whose brass buttons had an insignia which I did not recognize, dark grey flannel trousers and suède shoes. He was English.

"Indeed yes," I answered. "At Klébers in the Rue Royale."

Then he was sitting down and the glass was on the table six inches away from mine.

"I have some friends who are most anxious to meet you, Mr. Graham," he said.

"I'm quite at a loose end. I've no doubt that would be delightful." I had flushed something here all right.

"I'm so glad you think so. Had you decided differently I might have been compelled to take other

29

measures." He looked over my shoulder and smiled. He had practically no lips at all.

Turning in my seat I followed the direction of his glance. At the table behind me were two of the biggest and toughest Frenchmen I had ever seen in my life.

"I assure you that they could have managed it quite easily and without disturbance," the man in the smoked glasses said. "They are, after all, experts. However, I'm so glad that it is not necessary. Shall we go?"

I finished my drink and stood up. We left the café chatting amiably.

"You flew, of course," my companion said, and we discussed air-travel until we reached a *traction avant* drawn up by the kerb. The man in the smoked glasses got in behind the wheel and beckoned me to sit beside him. The two thugs sat in the back.

The *traction avant* has always had slightly sinister connotations for me. It had been the favourite motor car of the Gestapo during the Occupation and three of them had once chased me round Tours. The two thugs in the rear seat brought the whole thing unpleasantly back to me. My mouth went dry and I began to call myself all sorts of a fool for letting myself in for this. Then I took a pull on myself and concentrated on where we were going.

Smoked glasses, as I had mentally christened him, sent the car through the traffic with great speed and skill. We climbed the Champs-Elysées, crossed the Etoile, tore down the Avénue Foch and into the Bois.

Across the Bois we went with the needle on sixty, through the Porte de Boulogne, across the little Place and into the streets beyond.

A minute or two later we pulled up at a house in a street I didn't know. The door was opened immediately and we went inside. It was, I guessed, one of those streets which had been run up in a hurry in the thirties. The houses were very much of that decade—after Le Corbusier, all windows and straight lines. We went up the curving stone stairs and into a long room on the first floor. The bodyguard, I noticed, remained below.

The room was rather charming; it ran the whole length of the house and the street side was, as I had expected, mostly glass. The floor was polished parquet; there were bright rugs, a bookcase with French and English novels, an Adam card-table with a comprehensive array of drinks on it and some goodish-looking pictures which I didn't recognize. In the far corner was a grand piano at which a man was sitting. I still remember the shock of disappointment when I saw that it was not Rupert.

He was a man of medium height, squat, ugly and dark-jowled. The first impression which I had of him was that he looked like a toad and I then and afterwards thought of him as Mr. Toad of Toad Hall. He had stubby, ugly fingers and he was playing Cole Porter's "Night and Day". He looked up as I came in. "Give him a drink, Shelby," he said, in a throaty, croaking voice.

"I'll mix some martinis," the man in the smoked glasses said.

"Thanks," I said. "But I've been drinking champagne cocktails. I'll stick to them if you can run to it."

Mr. Toad cocked an eye at me. "Quite at home, aren't you?" he said. Without waiting for an answer he turned back to his playing. The backs of his hands were covered with thick, dark hair. There was an air of power in repose about him. Although he spoke English perfectly I did not think he was an Englishman.

Shelby gave me a drink, a champagne cocktail in a goblet. He had not forgotten the slice of orange. It was a very good drink for which I was glad for I was beginning to think that I might need it.

Mr. Toad finished his playing and swung round to face me. "Your name", he said without preamble, "is Richard Graham. You are a moderately successful amateur steeplechase rider. You have enough money on which to live comfortably. You bet very little. Your trainer's bills are promptly paid. You do not owe money to tradesmen or to the bank. Since an unfortunate experience some years ago you have not become emotionally involved with a woman. You have no close relatives and few ties. Your summers are mostly spent abroad. You rarely communicate with anyone while you are abroad."

"Very accurate and efficient," I said. "Where is Rupert Rawle?"

He made a gesture of his hand as if to brush away a

matter of no importance. "Rupert Rawle is dead."

"He writes uncommonly good English for a dead man," I said.

The expression on the other man's face did not change. "Through a blunder on the part of someone who has since been called to account a typescript on which Rawle's name had been given as author found its way to you. This was unfortunate for both of us. I confess that to have a stupid young Englishman blundering about attempting to lay a ghost of his past or some such nonsense could prove a nuisance just now. I give you no more than that, Graham—just nuisance value. I think that I would be treating you kindly were I to offer you a sea cruise for two months in the Pacific. You would have every reasonable luxury. Should you desire it I can arrange that you do not go unaccompanied. I will even go so far as to see that you have a certain choice of companion—indeed by trial should you so wish. Naturally you will be under surveillance, but it will be as unobtrusive as possible. Does the offer appeal to you?"

Two months, that was interesting. Obviously they wanted me out of the way. If they were up to something and the book had more meaning than appeared at first, then whatever was on would break in the next two months.

"Sorry," I said. "I'm not interested."

"I see. Then, you foolish young man, you compel me to take other measures. You have come here alone and unaccompanied. Shelby was not followed. You will be taken to Bordeaux and given, penniless and unknown, into the hands of a captain of a cargo steamer. Whether you return from the trip with him will be for him to decide."

I had no doubt at all that he meant what he said. Luckily I had anticipated something like this and had prepared for it.

"I am afraid that ship will sail without me," I said. "You don't surely think I'd be foolish enough to walk in here without taking some precautions? A friend is to ring me at my hotel at varying hours throughout the night. If for any reason I do not answer he is to start right away in tracing me. He will have no difficulty following my movements to Kléber's. Shelby picked me up at a busy time. I don't think there will be much trouble tracing him. That is, of course, if you put this plan of yours into operation." I looked at my watch. "In fact it is almost time I was going." I was bluffing. This was an elaboration of my conversation with Saunders. But Toad couldn't know that and I doubted if he would risk calling me.

He stared at me unblinkingly for fully half a minute before he spoke. "One of your generals, Graham," he said, "Wellington, I think it was, said that he never made plans but kept ideas like bits of rope in his head and knotted them as he went along. You were a fool to turn down my offer. There is a corollary to the statement that every man has his price, and that is that every man can be frightened—somehow." He had been playing with something in his fingers as he was speaking. He stood up. "Take him back to his hotel, Shelby," he said over his shoulder. In three strides he was across the room and out through a pair of double doors which he closed behind him. As he passed me he threw in the air what had been in his hand. I caught it. In my palm was lying a piece of string with a knot in it.

Shelby and I stared at each other across the room.

"The George V, isn't it?" Shelby said.

As I nodded I examined him. He was a tall, thin chap. Although I could see no bulge under his coat it was almost certain that he was wearing a gun. Yet I felt that if I could get near enough to him I could probably take him. As if guessing my thoughts he smiled at me. It wasn't a friendly smile. "In case you are thinking of trying anything on," he remarked, "just look behind you."

I turned. One of the thugs had come in and was standing about a yard away. He grinned at me, revealing a row of blackened teeth. His breath, heavy with garlic, hit me like a blow in the face.

In the car we were in the same positions as before, Shelby and I in the front, the two thugs in the back.

I was half-expecting it when it came. Some distance inside the Bois the car slid to a stop. I had been right about the gun. Shelby leaned towards me. His hand flickered towards his left armpit and a gun appeared in it. It was a stubby, workman-like gun, a cut-down ·38.

It could blast my stomach through my back with no more noise than a blow-out or a backfire.

"Get out," Shelby said.

The four of us moved into the woods, Shelby just in front, I in the middle and the two thugs behind.

I glanced over my shoulder. Neither of the thugs had their hands in their pockets. They might or might not be carrying guns. Probably not. It was worth risking anyway.

I took a step backwards and swung as hard as I could with my right heel. It caught the left-hand thug exactly where I wanted it—smack in the middle of his shin-bone. It made a noise as if someone had stepped on a dry branch. He howled. The other one dived at me and I chopped him, downwards, with the edge of my hand, behind the right ear. Then I ran. There were shouts behind me and noises of heavy bodies in pursuit. They didn't lose any time so I hadn't damaged them much. They were tough all right.

What direction I should take I hadn't the faintest idea. My only object was escape. I thought I was getting away with it when one of the thugs by a lucky turn got almost up to me. He grabbed and missed. I did a rugby swerve, caught my foot in a root and came down. Without hesitation he threw himself on top of me. It was like being hit by the Empire State Building.

He got off me pretty quick and hauled me to my feet. The impact had just about knocked me out and I hadn't any breath left. Shelby was there with his gun in his hand. He hit me with it across the side of my face. Blood began to trickle into my mouth. The other tough hit me slam in the eye. My head went back and the man who was holding me grabbed my hair. I heard Shelby laugh and once more the gun came down. The pain was excruciating. I saw a big fist coming up. I could do nothing to avoid it. That was it. I went out.

I can't have been unconscious for very long. When I came to I was back in the *traction avant* and Shelby was cursing one of the thugs for letting me go out. The other was forcing neat whisky down my throat.

"All right, he's conscious," Shelby said.

The thug took the neck of the whisky bottle out of my mouth and poured the rest of the spirit over the front of my clothes. A wave of nausea hit me. I fought it down and slumped in the seat.

Shelby let in the clutch and drove to the George V. They hauled me out and propped me up. I heard Shelby explaining that I had been beaten up in a *boîte*, and adding something about, "Foolish young Englishmen."

We went up in the lift. They came into my room and shut the door behind them. "This is only a foretaste," Shelby said. "You will leave Paris tomorrow, go back to your ordinary life and forget about our affairs. You know now what will happen if you don't." He propped an envelope against the looking-glass. "That is your air-ticket. It gives you until tomorrow evening. You

37

•

may not feel like moving until then." He looked at me and laughed.

"Take your ticket to hell, damn you," I summoned up enough strength to say.

I saw Shelby nod to one of the thugs. A fist came from nowhere and hit me a tremendous slam which knocked me kicking into a corner. Then they went.

When I could I crawled to the loo and was sick. Then I got my head under the shower. That gave me strength enough to strip off my clothes. After that I staggered into the bedroom, took a secconal and just got into bed before I went out like a wick.

It was twelve o'clock the next morning before I awoke. For a few moments I could not remember what had happened to me. Then it all came back. I had once fallen in front of the field at Plumpton, at the fence on the top of the hill. They had galloped over me and played football with me. I felt now much as I had then.

Slowly and painfully I got out of bed and went into the bathroom. There wasn't much of me unbruised, but nothing was broken and my essential guts were still there, which was a relief. Most of the damage was in my face. My left eye was completely closed. I could see out of my right but it was all the colours of the rainbow and cuts and caked blood were everywhere. The idea of this, I suppose, was to combine the maximum of embarrassment with the maximum of deterrent effect.

After a quarter of an hour I had cleaned up my face

as best I could. The pistol had done most of the damage. The right side was practically raw.

I sent for the floor valet and gave him my clothes. Then I ordered a double dry martini, a ham omelet and a half a bottle of Pouilly Fuisse, the dry martini to come up quick.

When I had finished the martini I felt a bit better. It was not likely that my line in the George V would be tapped so I telephoned Morel. I told him what I wanted. He had done this sort of thing for me before and we arranged where to meet. Then I fell on the omelet.

While the boy was clearing the luncheon things away I put on a clean shirt and trousers. I was in the act of pulling on my tie when I felt rather than heard her behind me. It was her scent, I think. It hadn't changed. I knew instinctively that it was she. She must have come in as the boy was taking out the plates. I got the knot over the stud, pulled it straight and turned to face her.

She hadn't changed either. There it all was, the almost plain face, the wide, mobile mouth that set it alight, that gave it character and charm, the superb carriage, the long elegant legs, the clothes that came from Dior.

"Well, Jacquie," I said. "Well."

"Oh, Richard," she said. "What have they done to you! Your face!" She put out her hands to me.

I put my hands behind my back. "Your friends", I said, "have a quaint idea of plastic surgery."

"Richard, you must go. You must do what they want. They'll kill you if you don't."

"They will if they can, which is quite another matter."

She took a step nearer to me and lifted her hand to touch my cheek. I caught her fingers and pulled them away.

"Why did you do it?" I asked.

"What do you mean, Richard?" Her eyes opened wide in the way I knew so well.

"Go off with Rupert, you bitch." I was breathing hard, crushing her fingers under mine.

"Because we wanted to," she said simply.

"So you walked out on me and ran away with a traitor?"

"Yes," she flared. "And I'd do it again. He heightened things. He made you feel you were alive. You know it. You were in love with him yourself."

"Damn you I wasn't——"

"Call it what you will, it's the same emotion. You stupid English, you call it hero-worship or some such rubbish. You know what it was like—once Rupert wanted you he bewitched you. You know it because the spell is still on you, Richard. That is why you are searching for him now. You foolish boy, go home and forget us both. Go home, Richard. Richard, dear. I'd almost forgotten how fond I was of you all those years ago." She was very near to me. Her other hand came up and stroked my face.

For a second I thought that I was going to hit her. Then, as I looked down at her, at the red mouth and the body I had so often longed for, a tremor of passion ran through me. I pressed her arm behind her and drew her towards me. Her body bent willingly to mine.

Minutes later she pushed me away. "This is madness," she said. "They don't know I'm here. I heard them talking. I know they'll kill you, Richard, if you stay. Richard, Richard, darling, none of us, neither I nor Rupert, means anything to you now. Go home. Go back to your sensible English life, go back to letting horses try to kill you." She laughed and stroked my cheek again.

"Rupert is alive, isn't he?" I asked.

"Forget us both, dear Richard." She kissed me, once, lightly on the lips, and then she was gone. Nothing remained but the fragrance of her scent in the air.

I glanced at my watch. I hadn't much time if I was to see Morel and still catch the aircraft. For I was getting out. I was going back to London to pick up the threads of my normal life. As Toad had said every man has his point of turning back where fear is concerned. I had reached mine; I had had enough. At least that is what I wanted them to think. In fact I meant to return to France and that as soon as I could. For Rupert was alive, of that I was now quite sure. And I had an idea that I knew where I might find him.

I took a taxi to the Rue de La Paix. That I was sure to be followed did not bother me. They could not follow me into the room to which I was going.

At my destination I went up to the top floor in a gilt and crimson lift. Walking almost ankle deep in a lush cream carpet between tall, cream walls I came to a door at the end of a corridor. I knocked, turned a shapely gilt handle and went in. It was a small room, richly furnished—too richly for my taste. At a superb ormolu-mounted desk a tall, cadaverous-looking man was sitting. Beside him stood Morel.

The tall man turned an ornate key in the top of the desk and slid up the tambour front. He reached inside and handed me a rectangular brown paper parcel. There was a sheet of writing paper on top of it. I scribbled my name on this and gave it back. The tall man glanced at it, folded it in two, nodded to Morel and left the room.

Breaking open the parcel I took out the thick wad of 10,000-franc notes which was within. Stripping ten from the top I pushed them across the desk to Morel. "Listen carefully," I said. "This is what I want you to do." As I talked I broke the notes up into small packets and distributed them between various pockets. When I returned to France I didn't want to be bothered by shortage of cash or by currency regulations. "Will that be enough?" I said, as I finished speaking.

"It will do. You still think that Rupert is alive and that you can find him?"

"Yes. If you know anything that will help me you might as well tell it to me now."

He gave a faint shrug. "You seem to know far more than I do, my friend. I, too, would like to meet him again—if he lives. But you have been in the wars since I saw you last night."

"Yes, and I think I have probably been followed. I shall want to use the escape."

"That will be easy. But you must get treatment for that face. I shall take you to someone not far away."

We walked along the corridor until we reached a blank end wall. Here Morel pressed a spring in the panelling and a section slid aside. It was an old Resistance doorway. "They still have their uses," Morel said, with a smile.

We walked casually through the other shop and into the crowded street.

My face was hurting damnably now and the salve and bandages which the chemist supplied were a wonderful ease. I collected my bag at the hotel, told the taximan to drive me directly to Le Bourget and said good-bye to Morel. He had asked no further questions nor had I vouchsafed any more information. I wondered idly as the taxi took me along how much of the hundred pounds would find its way into his pockets.

I was sitting in the *salle d'attente* waiting to be called to the aircraft when someone took the chair next to me. I looked up. It was Shelby.

"You have been in an accident, my poor friend," he said. "Nothing serious, I hope."

"It wasn't an accident and perhaps it's serious, perhaps not. It depends on how you look at it."

"At any rate I am sure you will find that you recover quickly in London where there will be no likelihood of a recurrence."

"That is just the possibility I'm guarding against," I said.

"How wise. I'm so glad you took our advice."

I suppose he never knew how near he was to being knocked for six off his chair, his smoked glasses smashed and his thin lips pushed into his teeth. I might have lost my temper and done it and ruined everything, but at that moment we were called.

As we boarded the aircraft I looked over my shoulder. He was still there, at the edge of the tarmac, watching me.

We taxied out, turned down the runway and took off. I saw Sacré Coeur, its spire and cupola piercing the evening mist. It disappeared below and then we had left Paris behind and were climbing through the clouds towards the Channel.

I settled back in my seat and began to think. Already, even then, I had in my mind the first faint beginning of a guess as to what had taken Rupert away.

Three

ROUGH SHOOTING IN THE MAURES

At London Airport I rang up Saunders's flat. My own phone would, I felt sure, have been tapped by now for this was a precaution Mr. Toad and Co. would hardly overlook. In any event I was not going to risk using it for the purpose I had in mind.

Saunders was not in but his housekeeper told me that he was dining at the Garrick Club and that I would probably find him there. I got through to the club and then had to wait for the hell of a time before he came to the phone. When he did come on he did not seem pleased at being disturbed. "Well, what do *you* want?" he asked in a very disgruntled tone.

It was essential for my purposes that I should try to placate him. What I wanted was that he should do something for me and I did not know how he was going to take it.

"I'm frightfully sorry if I've hauled you out of dinner," I said, pushing down the charm stop as far as it would go. "I wouldn't have bothered you only it is terribly important."

"Very well, what is it?" He seemed slightly mollified. "You haven't been killed, anyway."

"I've been beaten up from hell to breakfast. You ought to see me."

"What?" He seemed interested now. "There was something in it, then. Have you got the typescript back?"

"No, but I've got something that will interest you. Can you meet me at Kempton Park tomorrow afternoon?"

"Kempton Park! Good God! That's a race meeting, isn't it? I've never been to one in my life. Don't be ridiculous, Graham. Come round to my flat later on if you like."

"I can't do that. I'm sure I'm being followed. I shouldn't stay much longer here, either."

"No more can I. I'm dining with Percy Trover and I think he is going to leave Harvey and James. I can't waste any more time with you, Graham."

"Pompous Percy! Look—I know him. He has a few jumpers with Pat Kendrick. I rode a winner for him at Cheltenham last year. And listen, Saunders, he is more or less certain to be at Kempton tomorrow. You could clinch the deal there. Anyway, it'll do you no harm to meet him racing."

"How do you get on with him? Can I mention your name?"

"He gave me a pearl pin. I was hoping for a motor car."

46

"What on earth are you talking about?"

"You'd better learn the language, Saunders. You'll never get Pompous Percy on to your list if you don't. Racing is a sort of religion with him. Yes, mention my name—it might do you a bit of good."

"Are you serious about his racing?"

At that I knew I had him. "Of course I am. It's O.K. about Kempton, then? Two o'clock in the upstairs bar. Don't on any account phone my flat. I'll have a voucher sent round to you."

"What the dickens is a voucher?"

"Ask Pompous Percy," I said, and hung up.

By the time I got back to the flat I was pretty whacked, but I still had a lot to do. First I searched for and eventually found a rough sketch map of certain tracks in the Maures which I had made when I had been searching the country after Rupert's reported death. I glanced at it and put it in my wallet. I could memorize it on the plane going out. Then I sat down and wrote out in the fullest possible detail what had happened to me and what I had guessed about what was going on. It wasn't much at that stage, but it was something. Luckily I had some flimsy paper and, writing as small as I could, I got it all on to a couple of sheets. These I put into an envelope which I addressed to Saunders.

It was late when I had finished. I set the clock which makes my tea for an early call and turned in. Next morning I went to my club where I telephoned for a seat on a plane to Nice. The club line could hardly be tapped nor could its correspondence very well be interfered with. I arranged for the tickets to be sent there. After that I wrote to George Verschoyle, told him I was going away and sent him a cheque to cover what expenses he might have with the horses for the next couple of months. Like most trainers George is almost always about to go on the rocks and I didn't want him stuck with the keep of my horses if anything happened to me. I also wrote to my solicitors telling them if I didn't show up in a couple of months to open my will and get in touch with Saunders. I thought it would be a nice touch if I made Saunders an executor, but I hadn't time to go round and get them to draw the necessary codicil. I gave the letters to the hall porter and then I went out to Kempton.

Of course the first people I met on the stairs were George and Mary Verschoyle.

"Good lord, what have you been doing to yourself?" George asked.

"I hurt myself riding work," I said, this being the best lie I had been able to think up to answer the inevitable question.

"I can guess the sort of work that was," George remarked.

"I suppose the horse's name was Angry Husband," Mary said tartly.

I spotted Saunders the moment I entered the big bar. He was at the sandwich counter in the middle of the room and he looked as out of place as a games mistress at a St. Tropez night-club. Come to think of it I had seen a games mistress on the Isle de Levant and she looked pretty much at home, but perhaps that was different.

Saunders did not look at home here. He had put on the sort of tweeds he used for week-end visiting. They were very much the Londoner's idea of what ought to be worn in the country and were as stiff and pressed as if they had been made of cardboard. In addition he was wearing a green hat with a feather in it which I think he must have bought in Austria. His hands were thrust into his trouser pockets. From the expression of extreme wariness on his face I guessed that they were firmly clutching all his available money. He did not hear me approach and when I tapped him on the shoulder he jumped.

"Your hunter awaits you in the silver ring," I said. "Or perhaps I should say chamois. Just one yodel is required to make you the toast of Kempton Park."

"I say! What extraordinary people! What does that little man do?"

"Everyone he can if he gets the chance. I see you haven't a racecard." I slipped the letter between the leaves of the card in my pocket and put it on the counter beside him. "There is a letter addressed to you in that card," I said, still in a conversational voice. "I'm going away again tomorrow. If you don't hear from me within the time I've specified in the letter get in contact with the people at the address which I've also given you. Put all the information in the letter before them. It may be some help to them."

Saunders looked at me properly for the first time. "You've been beaten up, all right," he said. "This is exactly like something out of one of Maurice Merevale's novels. I hope there isn't any likelihood of it happening to me."

"No. You're much more likely to be murdered."

"What! Now, look here, Graham, this sort of thing is all very well to read about in one of Merevale's books, but I don't think——"

"Prepare to receive cavalry," I said. "Here is Pompous Percy. Don't get rattled. Mind your blood-pressure. One false step and you've lost him."

He bore down on us, the covert coat with its velvet collar swinging open over his vast stomach, the grey homburg at the famous tilt, the gold-mounted cane at the carry. "Ah, Graham," the celebrated fruity voice which had charmed millions over the B.B.C., flowed towards me like a syrup. "Waiting for the winter game, no doubt, ha."

"Precisely. You've put it in a nutshell," I said, bury-ing my nose in a glass of pale ale. As a matter of fact, like Saunders but for a different reason, I had no wish to antagonize him. He was a pompous windbag, but two of his chasers were good ones and I knew that he insisted on having a say in who rode them. Moreover a best-selling novelist and B.B.C. and television pet who spent his money supporting steeplechasing had many of his sins forgiven him, at least to my way of thinking.

"Quite different from some of the summer games he gets up to," Saunders said with, for him, unwonted asperity.

"I'm glad to meet you, Saunders," Percy continued, booming away. He never paid attention to what anyone else said, anyway. "About last night. I've been thinking things over. I rather want a word with you——"

This was my dismissal. I pushed off. Later in the day I saw Percy and Saunders together in the other bar apparently on most amicable terms so I supposed negotiations were going well. They had picked up Hugh Watson-Williams, the character actor. Probably Saunders was trying to get an option on his memoirs.

I had a fiver on one of George's horses which came up. Then, after racing, I went back to my club where I collected the air ticket and had dinner. When I had finished my meal I took a taxi to my flat, went upstairs and packed a bag.

After that came the business of leaving without being seen. I hadn't in the least minded being followed up to now nor did I object to my flat being watched. My movements had been studiously normal and innocent. But now came the time when I didn't want to be seen or followed. Well, whoever had stolen Rupert's book had shown me the way in. There seemed no reason why I should not use it to get out.

I went along the passage and eased up the window. It had looked very simple when I had given it a casual glance. Now, when I had to do it, and with a bag in my hand, the street seemed a long way down and the gap enormous.

Setting my teeth I put both my legs out the window. Thus I got on to the ledge on my side. I hadn't yet committed myself for I still had my right hand with the bag in it inside the window. I didn't like it a bit, but it was no use standing there like a fool and I didn't think I could balance myself much longer on that narrow ledge, anyway. So I stretched for it. I got my foot on the other ledge all right but I couldn't get a hand-hold. Worse, my hand with the bag in it was pulling me back. I thought I was going to be stuck there, straddled across the gap, between the street below and eternity. Then a stanchion met my grasping fingers. I pulled myself over sweating and gasping.

The far ledge wasn't all that easy. It was narrower than it looked and I had to go past a lighted window on my way. The curtains were not drawn but the occupants of the room were so occupied with what they were doing that they did not notice my passing. I could not help but see in so I gained some interesting information on the sex-life of S.W.1.

At last I reached the fire-escape and went down it. Nobody challenged me or interfered with me in any way. At Knightsbridge I got a taxi and drove to a quiet hotel in Kensington. There were, I guessed, a succession of long days and nights ahead of me. I went immediately to bed and slept straight through until I was called.

At eleven o'clock the next morning I was over northern France again. This time I was headed south for Nice. I had brought with me to read in the plane the latest Maurice Merevale and *The Daily World*. The newspaper was still plugging the split in Anglo-American relations. There had been another oil deal and their foreign correspondent had a middle page article entitled: "Are We Selling our Empire Too Cheap?"

During luncheon I put aside the thriller which I had been reading and took out my sketch map. It was really only a matter of refreshing my memory and I soon had the whole thing etched into my mind. I tore up the map and put the pieces on to my plate. After this there would, I felt sure, be no going back. This time was for keeps.

It was a lovely, cloudless day. I did not feel impelled to pick up the Maurice Merevale again. Instead I stared out at the far snow line of the Alps. In the distance I could see the peak of Mont Blanc sharp and clear against the pale blue of the sky. Below, the changing landscape of valleys, cliffs and crags offered always something new to the eye. I sat looking out, lost in my thoughts. I wondered if I should find Rupert, somehow I thought I should. But what would happen when I found him I refused to think about. The moment itself could take care of that.

When I looked at my watch I saw that in ten minutes we would be coming in.

The approach to Nice Airport is, I think, unsurpassed in Europe. One moment the Alps are around you in their beauty and splendour, the next the whole of that lovely coastline lies below. Then you are out over the sea circling, one wing down for the approach. The next moment you are flying alongside the Promenade des Anglais looking into windows and fancying you could stretch out a hand and pluck the toy people from the beach and the streets. Then there is the faint jolt of the landing and the aircraft is down. It is all as dramatic and colourful as the coast to which one has come. I love it.

As I stepped out of the aircraft the warmth came up and enfolded me like a cloak. I paused for a moment and looked about me, at the palms, the dazzling whiteness of the buildings, and the clarity of the colours on the hills behind. It was good to be back even on a mad mission like mine.

The customs did not delay me and I walked past the bus-ticket counter into the glare outside. Then I got a shock. Morel was standing ten yards from the entrance, watching it. I walked over to him. "I didn't expect you, Morel," I said. "Have you got the car?"

"I like to take care of important things myself, my friend," he answered. "And this seemed important."

He led the way to the car park. There he indicated

an open Jaguar XK 140. It was painted cream with red upholstery and red piping.

"My God, Morel," I said. "If you had decided to advertise my presence you couldn't have done it better. I didn't say I wanted something straight from Hollywood."

"You asked for a car, *mon vieux*. I got you the best. You will find what else you wanted in the pocket of the driver's door."

I put my bag in the boot and got in behind the wheel. The engine started immediately.

"You are going to Cannes?" Morel said. "I will go with you as far as that."

I looked at him. "Does it matter where I'm going?" I said.

"Not really. I will be with you for a little way wherever your road lies."

I nodded and let in the clutch. He had the door open and was sitting beside me as the wheels took the drive.

I drove along the approach road to the airport and turned left on to the trunk road to Cannes. Once I had cleared the airport I let her go. We went across the dried-up Var with the needle touching ninety. At the most I reckoned I had twelve hours' start before the hunt was up. Sooner or later the watchers were going to wonder why I didn't leave my flat and then they were going to go in and find out. I wanted to waste as little as possible of those precious hours talking to Morel. Besides, as I've said before, I never knew how far I could trust him.

His appearance here with the car didn't encourage me to confide in him. He sat staring out through the windscreen, not speaking, all the way to Cannes.

I parked the Jaguar under the trees by the port. Morel got out, shut the door carefully and leant on it. "I think we had better have a talk," he said.

I looked at my watch. "If it doesn't take more than ten minutes."

We went to a little restaurant on the far side of the port and sat down facing the rows of yachts. It was not a drinking time and the place was empty except for an old man in a striped jersey and blue trousers drinking Pastis.

"Now then, Morel?" I said. "What is this all about?"

He took his time about answering. Finally he put the Caporal he was smoking into the ashtray between us and looked out over the port.

"I am a journalist," he said. "I live by the stories I find. I have helped you from time to time and asked no questions, but now, I think, is the time you pay me back. You are on to something, Graham. I think you have picked up Rupert Rawle's trail. It could be the story of the century. Do I get it?"

There was something in what he said. Without him I would not have been sitting here ready to seek and strive. He had helped me and, if he was on the level, he deserved to get the story. But even if he was on the level, until I had finished what I was going to do I would not cut him in.

"You told me Rupert was dead," I said. "What made you change your mind?"

"I haven't changed my mind. But there is what I think you call an outside chance that you may be right. I can't afford to pass it up."

"I don't know how warm the trail is. I won't know until after I have done what I want to do this afternoon. Where I'm going may be a blind alley. I don't know."

"Take me with you."

"No. If I find Rupert, and I don't say that I will, I want to meet him alone."

"Rupert may not be alone."

"I'll chance that."

"Very well. I'll wait for you here."

"For how long?"

"Until midnight."

"And if I don't come?"

Morel shrugged his shoulders. "You may be dead," he said. "In which case I must only follow your trail as best I can. You may be alive and holding out on me. But I wouldn't advise the latter course. I worked on the coast for three years. I know every inch of it and I have many friends. I shall find you, where ever you are. And remember, Graham, I have been a good friend. I can also be a bad enemy."

I took the back road over the hills from Cannes to Fréjus, cramming the Jaguar as hard as I could between the lorries and the business traffic. Certainly

Morel had picked the car well for his own purposes. He would not have much difficulty in tracing me if I let him down—up to a point at least, for I doubted if even his agents would find where I was going.

Beyond Fréjus I headed west along the coast, sending her flying down the straight stretch of road past the aerodrome. After covering some miles I left the main highway for a road which ran towards the hills. In about five minutes' driving I came to a fork. The road to the right led downward towards the plain. That to the left would bring me into the hills. I took the left-hand fork. Soon I was climbing steeply. The surface continued sound for about a mile and then it deteriorated into a mixture of bare rocks, holes and dry rivulets. Quite sizeable boulders stuck out here and there and in places the winter rains had carved deep trenches as they dashed down to the sea. All the time I was climbing. Before long the road became a mere track cut like a scar between the pines and cork oaks, clinging to the hill-side as best it could. Every now and then it would run straight for a few yards before gathering strength, as it were, to reach upwards again. In one or two places other tracks led off, going down to lonely farms in the valleys and cuttings. But I had memorized my map well and I held on my way.

After about half an hour I came to a ruined farm where four tracks crossed. I was high up now in the loneliest heart of the Maures. No tourists came here for the roads would not carry their cars. These tracks were not marked on Michelin maps nor were they sign-posted. If you came you came alone and found your own way. There was a little clearing here and far, far away, through a gap in the pines, I saw the sun flash on the sea.

Taking the track ahead of me I went on, but more slowly now for I was nearing my destination. The road became worse, if that were possible. It was now only two white wheel tracks for strong growths of box had sprung up in its centre. These rattled and brushed against the underside of the Jaguar. It was as well that I knew my way. Two hairpin bends, a right and a left, took me up to a straight stretch of road running for once on a gentle downward slope. Putting my foot on the brake I brought the car to a standstill. I had found what I was looking for.

Built on a spur of the Maures running out into a little valley it lay in the sun, a long, low building of bleached white stone roofed with the red tiles of the country. This had been Rupert's hiding-place.

The end gable of the house rested on the very extremity of the spur. Below it, cut out of the hill itself, was a small sheltered terrace. It was this terrace which gave the building the look of an animal at rest and which had earned it its name—"The Crouching Lion".

During the latter half of the nineteenth century a wealthy Parisian had built the house as a retreat. His wife had died tragically and there he had sought and found solitude. So well had the site been chosen that although through a gap in the Maures the house commanded a magnificent view of the coast and the sea, other shoulders and spurs shut it off everywhere from observation. Of all the tracks which led through the pines only one gave a brief glimpse of the house and that went to a deserted farm and was all but disused. In fact by now it had probably gone back to the forest. I knew all this because five years ago I had spent three days in the hills looking for the house. It was, of course, admirably suited to the purposes of Rupert's employers.

The Frenchman's architect had managed to create a miniature park on the side of the spur facing me. Cypresses grew there and once there had been trim lawns and gardens, a tiny lake and a fountain. The cypresses were there still but the rest of the park looked desolate and uncared for.

All about me was quietness. Nothing moved. Only the faintest of hill-breezes sighed through the pines. Pushing myself up on to the back of the seat I sat looking at the house. The shuttered windows stared blankly back at me. All around was the sweet smell of the pines. A great bird from the higher hills came swooping and planing down the valley. The *cigales* clacked their endless chorus. There was no other sign of life. The house slumbered in the heat.

For thirty minutes I sat there, watching. Then I slid down behind the wheel and took off the brakes. The Jaguar ran forward. Fifty yards further on was a place which I had found before where some long-forgotten landslide or else workmen seeking material for the house had hollowed out a portion of the hill. I turned the car through the screen of branches. They closed behind her. She was as well hidden as if she had been in a room.

Putting my hand into the door pocket I took out the Luger. It had been used before, I noticed, as I saw the wear on its butt, and it fitted snugly into my hand. I made sure that it was loaded and that the action worked and then dropped it into my pocket. Parting the screen of trees I went quietly through the stillness and the sun, down the track to the house.

The wrought-iron gates of the park with their tracery of the crouching lion were firmly shut. The locks were rusted and the iron cracked and uncared for. But the wall beside them was full of footholds and handholds for it was rotten and crumbling. I went up it as if it had been a ladder.

The drive was overgrown, the grass of the park long and coarse and yellow; the watercourse was rank with weeds, the fountain broken and silent. A balustrade bordering a flagged path ran along this side of the house.

I climbed the balustrade and dropped on to the flags. As I did so, quite clearly and near at hand, I heard the bark of a dog. At the same time I saw that the windows opening on to the terrace were not shuttered. When I had watched from the road these had been hidden from me by the wall of the park. They were french windows and one or two stood open. The dog barked again.

I took the Luger in my hand and stepped through one of the open windows. The room inside was long and cool and dark. The furniture was covered in dust-sheets and there was a smell of disuse in the air. Crossing to the door I opened it gently. It gave on to a large bright hall, painted and pillared, with a gallery running round it. The sides of the gallery reached to a dome in the roof. On the left was a graceful staircase of shallow stone steps. This split into two branches half-way up, the branches leading to the gallery.

There was no one about. I crossed the hall and made for the staircase. I thought that the sound of the dog's barking came from the far side of the house. There was a big window lighting the staircase where the branches divided and this seemed a good vantage-point from which to spy out the land.

When I got to the window I found myself looking down into a small courtyard. The dog was there all right. He was chained by a staple to the wall of one of the buildings. He was a big, black mongrel with white markings, some sort of Great Dane cross, I thought, and an ugly customer if he didn't like you.

As I watched, an old man in a smock came from below me and walked towards a pair of double doors in the opposite wall. He freed the retaining bar, pulled up the bolts and opened the doors. A Land Rover rolled into the courtyard.

Two men got out of the front of the Land Rover. They were Mr. Toad and the gunman, Shelby. The dog set up a racket the moment it saw Shelby, jumping to the end of its chain, pulling to try to get away, barking and growling. The old man quietened him.

Then, out of the back of the car, a third figure descended. I recognized him immediately and I heard my breath escape in a hiss of excitement. At this distance he seemed to have changed not at all since I had last seen him. There was the same swashbuckling, almost rolling gait of those slightly bandy legs, the same impish look on his face. . . . I even heard the well-remembered chuckle and his infectious laugh. So Rupert Rawle was not dead. That was one problem solved, anyway. He was very much alive and on terms with Mr. Toad and Shelby.

Then I saw that the old man in the smock was talking excitedly to the other three men. He pointed to the dog and they all turned to look at the house. I drew back quickly. It was time I was getting out. I could watch better now from the woods.

I went down the stairs, crossed the hall and the sheeted, silent room, went over the balustrade and down through the thick, coarse grass of the park. Then I was up and over the wall and had landed panting in the road. Opposite me was a clear stretch of grass such as you sometimes see in those hills. It was, I suppose, about fifty yards wide. I had to cover those fifty yards to get to the safety of the trees. I took a deep breath and ran for it.

I thought I had made it. I could only have been ten yards from the trees when the shot rang out. The noise and the impact were almost simultaneous.

My right foot felt as if it had been kicked from under me and I came down in a heap. But I had been under fire before. I rolled over as I fell, pushed myself sideways and then dived head first for the firs. Another shot tore through my shirt as I went. Shelby was making nice shooting but he wasn't having the best of luck.

Behind the screen of trees I found a dry watercourse and went down it on my knees and elbows. After about thirty yards I cautiously raised my head. I was out of sight of the house and of the road. Around me was a carpet of pine needles and fir cones were lying about. It seemed safe enough and I started to get to my feet.

When I put my right foot to the ground I keeled over and collapsed. I had quite forgotten that I had been hit. I didn't feel any pain and there was no blood about that I could see. Sitting up I pulled my leg on to my knee to have a look at it. When I saw what had happened I laughed. Shelby had indeed had bad luck. The heel of my right shoe had been neatly sliced off; there was a long rip in the loose part of my coat and my shirt. Neither bullet had touched me.

Making for the Jaguar I hobbled on. She was where I had left her. The engine fired immediately. I backed her on to the road and swung the wheel hard down to have her facing the right way. As she straightened I slammed the lever into first. Then I looked up. Ten yards away the Land Rover was across the road.

Four

A LESSON IN CANASTA

Standing in front of the Land Rover was Shelby. There was a smile on his lipless mouth and a sporting rifle lay in the crook of his arm. "Come out with your hands up. That is if you can walk," he said.

I opened the door and limped up the road towards him.

"Where did I hit you?" he asked, with an air of professional interest.

"You didn't. You got the heel of my shoe."

"And the second?"

I looked down at the tear in my coat and made a movement with one hand to indicate it.

"Don't drop your hands." He spoke sharply. "There must be something wrong with this ruddy rifle. I was beginning to think I'd have to go in and get you."

He didn't sound as if he had liked that thought and I made a mental note that his nerve might not be as good as his eye. I cursed myself, too, for not having stayed there and waited for him.

"Gaston," Shelby called, without moving his gaze from me. "Come here."

The old man in the smock came out from the trees behind me. He had a sawn-off shot-gun in his hands. It was as well that I had made no move to try to go for Shelby.

"Get his gun," Shelby commanded. "And see that you don't get in my line of fire, you old dotard."

The old man knew what he was doing. He reached in at arm's length and plucked the Luger out of my pocket.

"Throw it into the Jaguar and then back it off the track," Shelby ordered.

This was done with much grinding of gears and a running fire of snarls from Shelby. Then the old man rejoined us on the road.

"Get into the driver's seat of the Rover and you, Graham, get in beside him." Shelby sat in the back and rested the rifle on the top of my seat. Its muzzle just touched my back. "Even with this so-called shooting-iron I could hardly miss you at this range," he remarked conversationally.

We drove down the road and into the courtyard. The dog set up a racket again the instant he saw Shelby. The gunman cursed back at him as we walked towards the house. The last I saw of the dog he was leaping at the end of his chain, barking and snarling.

I was brought into the hall and along a lofty passage. Shelby opened a door and motioned me inside.

It was a long room at the very end of the house. Three tall windows looked on to the balustraded terrace and the little park. Opposite me another window set in the end wall opened on to the hanging gallery which gave the house its name. At present the room appeared to be used as a combined living-room, dining-room and office. A scrubbed refectory table ran alongside the windows. In a corner was a tall marquetry bureau, its desk littered with papers. There was an ornate nine-teenth-century chimneypiece, a sofa covered in blue material with white piping and some modern chairs. In one of these sat Mr. Toad. A portable wireless set was on a small table beside him. He was listening to dance music from Radio Monte Carlo. There was no sign of Rupert.

Mr. Toad looked up as I entered. His squat face was quite expressionless but again I was struck by the air of power which emanated from him.

"I don't see my old friend Rupert Rawle," I said. 'Where is he? Hiding behind the arras?"

"So", Toad said, "you are still convinced he is alive?"

"I could scarcely disbelieve my own eyes, could I? I saw him getting out of the Land Rover."

"If you wanted to go on living you should not have told me that. Stories of messages left with your friends will not help you here."

"They may come just the same."

"No one", he said quietly, looking at me, his squat,

swarthy face still expressionless, "finds a grave in these lonely hills."

"What if I take up the offer you made me in Paris?" I was keeping talking, partly because I was frightened, partly because I was playing instictively for time.

"It is withdrawn. I gave you your warning, Graham. You saw fit to ignore it. I am going now. I have work to do. Work, if it interests you, with which the name of Rupert Rawle is vitally concerned. Keep an eye on him, Shelby. He is not, perhaps, as harmless as he looks. That is an invaluable attribute in those who wish to be dangerous. I may have underestimated you, Graham. Not that it matters now. When I return, you will die." He snapped off the radio and left the room. He had a flair for dramatic exits.

His words and the threat they contained hung in the air. Suddenly, in the way one recognizes the inevitability of an operation seconds or perhaps minutes after the surgeon has pronounced sentence, I knew that I was going to be killed.

Shelby and I stood for a moment just as he had left us. I remember I stared at the hideous chimneypiece, foolishly, unseeing, my brain frozen. Then Shelby beckoned me and we went upstairs.

I was imprisoned high up in the back of the house. It was a fair-sized room furnished with a divan bed, an armchair and a maple-board dressing-table. A small, tiled bathroom led off it. The bedroom had only one window. From it I could look down into the courtyard or command a view of the rolling, wooded Maures. In the hazy distance I could see the long stretch of the coast and the deep blue of the sea. It would be somewhere near Saint-Aygulf, I thought.

There was a window in the bathroom but it was too small and set too high in the wall to be of any use for the purpose of escaping. The one in the bedroom was not much better. Below was a sheer drop to the courtyard; above a good ten feet of smooth stone led upwards to the guttering of the roof. Nowhere was there the slightest indication of anything which would be useful as a toe or a handhold. Even if there had been I doubted my ability to use them. Richard William Chandos, that indefatigable escapee, would, no doubt, have found a way out from that window, but I was only a moderately successful gentleman rider and it was altogether beyond me.

I examined the fireplace and the floor and found nothing to help. Sitting on the edge of the bath I tried to remember an escape which I had read of in one of Maurice Merevale's books. Someone had sealed the bathroom and flooded it and used water power to sweep him to safety. It didn't seem at all practical to me and anyway I fancied that higher mathematics came into it somewhere which put it definitely out of my reach. Finally I gave it up, sat in the chair and stretched my legs and wondered what Morel would do, and if any succour could be hoped for from him.

My thoughts were interrupted by a bang on the door.

"Graham," Shelby's voice called.

"Yes," I answered.

"Stand back from the door."

"I'm in the chair thinking on beautiful things—like how I'd feel pushing your face in, for instance."

The door was kicked open, police fashion, and the old man came in carrying a tray of food. There was a bottle of wine on it which I was glad to see. Putting the tray down on the dressing-table the old man went out. Shelby lounged in the doorway.

"Do you want anything to read?" he asked.

"If you've got a complete set of Dornford Yates send it up. I might get some ideas about breaking out of here."

"Sorry, no Yates. There are a couple of Maurice Merevale's in Pans that people left behind them. I didn't imagine you'd want a thriller."

"All right. What else have you got?"

"Waugh, Greene, Anthony Powell, Maugham. The *New Yorker* if it interests you."

"Very middle-brow and pre-war. You're out of touch, chum. The backyard school is now all the go. You should have Amis and Wain and *Encounter*."

"You're a strange chap, Graham. I didn't think your sort could read."

"I'm a throw-back to the thirties—the last of the literary toughs. You ought to hear me quoting Proust in the weigh-room."

"*Swann's Way* is downstairs. Alakov reads it."

"So that is your boss's name, is it? Well, I'm not feeling very Proustian at the moment. I'll settle for *Brideshead Revisited* and some *New Yorkers*. There's a good racing page in the *New Yorker*, by the way. I can't think why Kingsley Martin doesn't put one into the *New Statesman*. I'd write it for him for a small fee. If you have a proof copy of Rupert Rawle's book you can send me that up, too."

His thin lips tightened. "One of the reasons I keep my job", he said, "is that I know nothing about anything and I ask no questions." The door shut and he was gone.

I wondered if he would punish me by not giving me the books, but in a few minutes he was back with an American edition of *Brideshead* and some copies of the *New Yorker*.

I took a bath and got into bed. There seemed nothing else to do. I tried to shut my mind to what was going to happen tomorrow and, to my surprise, I all but succeeded.

Opening *Brideshead Revisited* I started to read it for about the fifth time. Once more I found myself bewitched by the description of an Oxford I never knew. I found myself wondering if the twenties were really as gay and as glamorous as they were painted. If you were young and rich and well-connected then they probably were. But certainly some of their survivals looked pretty silly now. Anyway, it was all a far cry from a condemned cell far up in the lonely Maures.

Quite soon I found myself getting drowsy. Putting the book aside I stretched and turned over in bed. The French understand the importance of beds. Almost invariably they are sensuous and comfortable, ideally designed either for sleep or for love. This one was no exception. Automatically, it seemed, my limbs relaxed. In no time at all I was asleep.

It was early when I awoke. Sunlight was pouring through the window and flooding the room. It must have been the light on my eyes which had roused me.

The square of sky which I could see was that pale, hard, steely blue of the coast in the morning. I lay naked in the comfortable bed, slumbrous and relaxed, watching the sun creep across the room. Suddenly the realization of what was in front of me hit me and my mouth went dry.

Throwing aside the sheet I went over the room and the bathroom again, every inch of them. It was no good. The door was pitch-pine, thick and solid; the chimney was narrow and ran off at an angle into an-another flue.

After I had had my breakfast I went back to *Brideshead* but now the Gothic splendours failed to grip me. I tried the *New Yorkers*, but their sophistication in my present plight only made me cringe. I chucked them away and stationed myself at the window.

All was still in the courtyard. The big dog slept curled up in the sun, his chain coiled behind him. My eyes roamed the country-side. A stretch of the track ran past the house and curled to the left round a shoulder of the hill. Nothing moved on it, either. Far away an aircraft from Nice Airport droned towards the Alps. The slight morning breeze brought with it the sweet scent of the pines.

After about twenty minutes a door beneath me opened and the old man came out. Over his shoulder were a pickaxe and a spade. He crossed the courtyard to the double doors, opened a wicket in one of them and went out. I caught a glimpse of him on the track, then he turned off into the woods. I knew very well what he was doing and I felt fear come at me again and churn up my guts. It is not every day one sees someone about to dig one's grave.

Some time later Shelby appeared in the yard. The moment the dog saw him he came alive and angry, leaping to the end of his chain, snarling and barking. Like many of those long-legged dogs, he was a graceful brute, bounding and springing as if he was on rubber, keeping his feet and his balance against the remorseless tugging of the chain. Shelby snarled back at him, taunting him, deliberately provoking him. Then he, too, went out through the wicket and followed the old man into the woods.

Presently Shelby came back. He began to walk across the yard, his hands in the side pockets of his blazer. As he did so the dog once more started up. Shelby turned and cursed at him. Then it happened. What exactly was the cause of it I don't know. Perhaps the staple holding

the chain to the wall had never been securely fixed.
Perhaps the dog's incessant leaping and straining had
loosened it. At any rate it came suddenly free. The dog,
lips drawn back over his teeth, came on in the arc of his
leap straight at Shelby's throat.

The gunman took a step backward. His hand moved
to his armpit so fast that I hardly saw it. In a single
motion his hand was free again and with a gun in it.
Then came the crack of a shot. The dog's leap was
shattered in mid-air. A second later he was on the
ground a yard away from the man. He gave one con-
vulsive kick and then was still.

Shelby lowered the gun and looked at it. He reached
out his toe and touched the dog. It did not move. The
gunman remained for a few seconds staring down at the
body. Then he put the gun back under his arm and
went on into the house.

The body of the dog lay in the bright sunlight in the
yard. I waited for the old man to come back. It must
have been another ten minutes before the wicket gate
opened and he stepped into the courtyard. At first he
did not see the dog. When he did he stood stock still for
an instant. Then, dropping the pick and spade, he
ran shambling towards the body. He went on his knees
and took the dog's head in his hands. I saw his lips
moving and his hands fondling the dog. I looked
away.

When I came back to the window the old man and
the dog had gone.

Some years back I had broken my right arm schooling a horse for a friend of mine in Wales. It had been a couple of hours before they could get me to a doctor; by the time they did I was in considerable pain and they had to give me a general anaesthetic to put me out. It had been chloroform they had given me and a pretty heavy dose of it too, before they succeeded in getting me over. What with one thing and another I had had a baddish time and when they X-rayed the job the next day they found that something had gone wrong and the whole thing had to be done again. I remembered vividly the period of waiting for them to come for me and bring me to the theatre, and the sensation was much the same as that which I was now experiencing.

I had given up all hope of getting out and there was nothing I could do but wait. As when waiting for the anaesthetic the hours did not drag; on the contrary they sped away. They were my last hours and I wanted to save them and savour them, but they fled like minutes.

It seemed that I had barely turned from the window when lunch was brought. I had no more than finished eating—or so I thought, but my watch told me it was three o'clock—when there was a heavy kick on the door. It was followed by Shelby's shout telling me to stand back.

My knees were trembling. I cursed myself, stood up, swallowed and told him to come in.

He threw the door open. Then he leant against the

lintel, his hands in the side pockets of his blazer, staring at me through his smoked glasses. With a jerk of his head he indicated to me that I was to come out. "Straight along and down the stairs," he said.

He followed a couple of yards behind me and directed me to the room to which I had first been taken.

The old man was there laying out a tray of drinks. The portable radio had been moved and in its place a set of red and ivory chessmen had been set out. Some magazines and novels were lying about. One of the novels was Pompous Percy's latest, I observed with some amusement, and made a mental note to tell Saunders about this when I got back. Then my stomach cramped with realization. I wouldn't tell Saunders anything. I wouldn't see him again. I wasn't going back.

"We have to wait for Alakov," Shelby said. "I was bored stiff trying to read this stuff." He waved a hand towards Percy's book. "These modern novels are all balls. Do you play chess?"

"No," I said.

"Pity. What about cards? Gin-rummy? Canasta?"

"All right. Canasta then. How long have we got?"

"That depends on Alakov. In case you are thinking of trying something, Graham—Gaston, the oranges."

The old man shuffled over to a bowl which stood on a press by the wall. Taking three oranges from it he went towards the gallery at the end of the room. There he placed the three oranges on the balustrade about three inches apart.

"Hurry, fool. Get out of the way," Shelby commanded, an eager look on his face.

Once more the speed of his hand was blinding. It hardly seemed to move. Three shots rang out, deafening in the room. There was a sudden stink of cordite. I looked. The oranges had disappeared.

"Go on. Take a closer examination," Shelby said.

I went through the french windows on to the gallery. Involuntarily, when I got there, I took a step backwards. The balustrade was only knee-high, and there was nothing beneath it at all. It hung over space. Forty feet down the tops of the cork oaks showed.

Behind me Shelby chuckled. "No escape that way," he said.

Except for a dark stain of juice where the centre one had been there was no sign of the oranges. "Very impressive," I said to him as I came back into the room. "But you need not have bothered to put on this show. I saw you at work this morning."

He did not answer and I could see no change in his expression behind the big dark glasses.

While I had been on the gallery he had put out the canasta cards. He motioned me to sit opposite to him at the refectory table.

"I'm not taking any chances with you, Graham," he said. "For instance, you will deal for me and I shall play with one hand only leaving my right hand free. You have seen what it can do."

"Oh, yes. As I've said I'm most impressed." With my

knees I tested the table to see if there was any chance of heaving it on top of him. There wasn't. It was as solid as rock. "This is Rupert's old hideout, isn't it?" I asked him. "What is it now—a communist country club?"

"As a matter of fact we use it as a sort of clearing house. You'd be surprised at the number of people we have through one way or another. Some years ago we had two quite celebrated civil servants."

"If you mean who I think you mean I hope you gave them plenty to drink and let them sleep in the same room."

"They both got tight and had a most almighty row. I had to knock one of them cold. He was still a bit hazy when they took off the next morning. Cut for deal. I win."

"I suppose you were in one of the cloak-and-dagger shows during the war?"

He paused for a moment before answering. Then he said, rather reluctantly, I thought, "I had a staff job, as it happens."

"I see. And were you a traitor then?"

"Traitor is a strong word, Graham. Besides, I'm not one. I'm an employee. I've never sold any secrets, never given away any information. When I was in the army I found that I had an exceptional talent with firearms. No one, however, bothered to make use of it. After the war I took the trouble to perfect my skill. Again no one in my own country wanted my services.

I sold them to the highest bidder. It's a pleasant life —very little to do, really, and one lives on the best."

"I suppose it's much what they meant in medieval times when they spoke of selling one's soul to the devil. But the devil has a way of demanding his own—or so I've been told."

"That is a melodramatic way of putting it—I'm quite content. All my life I've wanted the best and here I get it. Women don't bother me much, but when I want one you'd be surprised at the beauty and talent in the bed which is at my disposal. I drink very little but when I need it it is there. The head waiters in the hotels of the international set know me and look after me. My clothes, cars and the tools of my trade all come custom built as the Americans say. It's a pleasant existence in return for some little services."

"I take back what I said before. Of course you're not a traitor. You haven't got the guts. You're a renegade."

"Hard words break no bones. At least I'm helping you to pass your last hours."

Yes, you swine, I thought, and all because you had nothing to read and were bored with your own company or perhaps, indeed, out of sorts for once with your own thoughts. There was something rotten at the core of him. He had had his snug staff job during the war and had then exploited his extraordinary gift. But I didn't think he would be much without his gun—or with it if someone was standing opposite him with another one. For the hundredth time I wished I could get those glasses off.

He played carefully and the game went slowly because of his insistence on playing with one hand. He leant his cards on a bulwark made of three novels stacked on top of each other and played them with his left hand. His right lay on the table between us, flat and menacing like the head of a snake. It fascinated me lying there, the fingers slightly curled. It was the only thing which stood between me and freedom for I knew that if I could pinion it I had him. But I also knew that it had all and more of the menace of a cobra for I had seen the speed and power of its strike.

At first I played mechanically not caring much about the game which I had at any rate to a great extent forgotten. He had to put me right concerning several minor points, about when one was allowed to meld and suchlike. He made me keep the score and he had to dictate the figures and the way of doing it to me, for this had completely gone from my memory. Moreover, he checked my figures and my tots each time to see that I hadn't made an error or was not cheating him.

Presently I began to take a greater interest in the game. For I had discovered that he was very anxious to win.

He was, it became very soon apparent, one of those card players who have what I think an almost pathological kink in that they cannot bear to be beaten even though no stakes are involved and nothing hinges on the game. When things were going well for him he was exultant; when they turned against him he became silent and glowering and inclined to curse the cards and his luck.

A still, small hope began to form in the back of my mind.

At first things went well for him. He ran away with the early hands and brought his score to over 4,000 without much trouble. At this time I was round the 2,000 mark—2,340 to be precise.

There was a smirk on his face. He was very pleased with himself. But he now had to have 120 to meld. My flicker of hope was turning a little brighter. The germ of an idea was forming in my brain. But the cards had to go my way if I were to put it into practice.

He put down two red threes after the next deal and the smirk grew more pronounced. I had a useful-looking hand. I had three kings, two tens, two jokers, no less than three twos and some odds and sods. I resolved to go for my canastas as quickly as possible and to stake all on getting out quickly and rattling him.

I did it.

I got the pack at the fourth discard with a ten, pulled another king and canastaed them with the jokers. I was now in a pretty strong position and he had not yet melded. I drew a red three and another wild two on the follow up. Immediately I made another canasta with the tens.

He didn't like this a bit. The smirk was now replaced

by a scowl. He wasn't liking what he was drawing, either. Two draws later I picked up yet another wild two. It was the sort of luck one dreams about. I had two fives and three sevens in my hand. I went out. He had not melded so he lost his two red threes.

When we totted up I was 4,310. He had a minus score, and that left him 4,200 even. We were both on 120 to meld. One or the other of us must get 5,000 and win on this hand. It was anybody's game.

I dealt the hands as slowly as I could, keeping him on the stretch. The moment I finished he snatched his cards up and started to arrange them against the books. He was frowning and fidgety, but he had not moved his right hand. I had to rattle him more. Alakov must surely return soon. This hand was my last chance.

He got the pack at my third discard and melded aces and jokers. It was a nice start to the last hand for he had not stripped his hand and had left himself plenty of cards to play with. This suited me, too. I fed him two small packs and he melded several more times—small melds which did not look dangerous from a canasta point of view. He thought he had me on the run and was building up his score.

He had melded three eights and from this he had held back at least one card in his hand for the eight of diamonds had been in the pack when he picked it up and it did not reappear on the table. No doubt this was to trap me into a discard. As it happened it was exactly what I wanted. He was being frightfully clever in his own mind as one is at cards when things are going one's way. The smirk came back.

Then I melded.

He didn't like that, but he went on steadily building up his own melds. He had no canasta and neither of us took the pack. It grew bigger and bigger. This, again, was what I wanted. I let go by two opportunities of taking it whilst I accumulated in my hand a collection of the denominations which he had on the table.

He began to cast hungry eyes on the pack and to swear beneath his breath when each discard denied it to him. Then he made a black canasta in tens. He had now in front of him three kings and a two, four eights, four sixes and a joker, three fives, three aces, four queens and another two.

He was getting into a dangerously strong position. I had to make my move now or not at all.

I froze the pack.

He looked at the joker I had laid across the upturned cards and muttered something under his breath.

I commenced to pelt him with the cards which he had on the table.

I was taking a chance that he might go out with his draws, but it was unlikely for he still had ten cards in his hand.

I made him hop. I threw two kings, two sixes, a queen, a ten, and a black three for good measure.

He was scowling hard and biting his lips. His discards gave me the pack twice, but I ignored them. I was playing my plan to the hilt.

The pile of cards had now grown to huge proportions. Whoever got it could not fail to win the game and, moreover, to mark up an immense score. I think there was a red canasta in it in fours alone.

I threw another king.

He was blind to everything except winning the game. Greed for the pack had bewitched him. He wanted it at that moment beyond anything else in the world. He had edged forward in his chair. His deadly right hand had moved in towards the cards.

This was it. Here was where I played my life.

I put my free hand into my cards and took out the eight of spades. Slowly, deliberately, I leant forward and laid it, face upward, on the discard pile.

I couldn't breathe. I daren't look at him. I must be right; I had to be. He must, he must be holding eights.

"Ah, ha," he said triumphantly. "Ah, ha."

His right hand stretched forward and grabbed the pack.

Five

LOVE IN THE VELVET NIGHT

I threw myself at him across the table. I got his gun arm and pushed it up, back and behind him. My right hand hit him where jaw meets neck. He smashed against the chair which tilted up with his weight. The great weight of the big table held it firm; his knees caught and he screamed with the pain of the impact. Then, together, we slid sideways to the floor.

I had him under me with his arm still behind him. His head hit first and then his arm. I heard it crack as the bone went. The big glasses came off and smashed on the floor.

For the first time I saw his eyes and then I knew that I had been right about him. They were pale, almost colourless, and now there was naked terror in them. He was only an arm and a gun. He screamed again, then his eyes filmed and he went out. He hadn't even struggled once his gun arm had gone.

Out of the corner of my eye I saw a sandalled foot two yards away from me across the floor. I was up in one motion, Shelby's gun coming out of its holster into my hand. Nothing was going to stop me now.

It was the old man, Gaston. He started back as the gun came up.

"*Doucement*, M'sieu, *doucement* . . ." he said.

He took a step nearer to where Shelby lay. Then, deliberately, he spat in his face. "*Sale cochon*. He kill Pedro, my dog, my friend—he kill him——"

"I know," I said. "I saw it."

"Listen, M'sieu, I hate him." He spat in Shelby's face again to emphasize his words. "I hate them all. I hear them talk. Sometimes he, Shelby, he talk to me when he is alone. He does not like to be alone too much, Shelby. He is afraid of himself, that one. You want to find the man who walks like this?" He moved across the room, imitating Rupert's bow-legged gait.

"Yes," I said. "That is right. I do."

"I tell you, M'sieu, where he is. He is in a village called Sainte-Marguerite. I think you know the Coast, M'sieu. They say you do. I hear them. You know Sainte-Marguerite?"

"Yes," I said. "I do. Where in Sainte-Marguerite is he? Is he in the village or the hills, or where?

"I do not know. All I know is that they talk of Sainte-Marguerite to him. And Alakov—he has much to do with Sainte-Marguerite, too."

"The man with the bow-legs—what is he doing there?"

"No, M'sieu, I know no more. I pick up a little here, a little there when they think I cannot hear."

"I see. What are you doing here if you hate them so?"

He looked me straight in the eyes. "I killed a man, M'sieu," he answered simply.

I glanced down at Shelby. He showed no signs of stirring. I touched him with my toe. "I want this tied up," I said.

"Yes. That is good. I will fetch some rope."

I hesitated for a second. Then I decided to trust him —at least that far. "All right. But hurry."

He was back in a minute with some strong cord of the type used for securing packing cases. He carried Shelby to a chair and lashed him into it.

"Now the problem is what to do with you," I said.

"It does not matter about me. I can tell them I have been busy away, when you do this——" he gestured towards Shelby.

"Yes, digging my grave, perhaps."

I don't know what expression I wore when I said that but the memory of those hours in the window had come suddenly and vividly back to me. Something of this must have showed in my face for the old man looked suddenly frightened. He didn't want to die, either.

What I was going to do didn't appeal to me much, but I felt that cricket was almost certainly not one of the old man's games. And, after all, only yesterday he had held a gun on me; this morning he had dug my grave.

"Turn round," I said.

Slowly, like a man with wooden legs, he got himself about, so that his back was towards me. He was beginning to buckle at the knees when I swiped him at the base of the skull with the butt of Shelby's gun.

I caught him as he fell and pulled him across to a chair. There I tied him up with the remains of the rope. It was a poor way of paying for the information which he had given me, but I didn't know how far I could trust him. In any event I was being cruel to be kind, for they could hardly suspect him of complicity in my escape when they found him lashed up and stowed beside their tame gunman.

When I had finished I took up the telephone and pulled it out by the roots. I slung the instrument over the balustrade and watched it sail into space. Then I thought I had better get out.

As I went down the passage to the hall I heard the clack-clack of heels on the tiles, coming towards me. The noise was very clear in the stillness of the house. Opening the nearest door I stepped inside. It was the same long room with the sheeted furniture which I had first entered from the park. Shafts of sunlight still shone through the windows on to the dust-covers. Closing the door until only a crack was left I took out Shelby's gun and held it against the opening. The heels came on. Whoever it was was in no hurry, sauntering along on a summer afternoon. Whoever it was would be in my field of view in a second. I tightened my grip on the gun.

She was wearing a white, flowered dress which swung about her as she walked. She had pushed her hat back and it was slung behind one shoulder. Her arms were slim and brown. She looked cool, unconcerned and quite charming. It was her wedge-heeled sandals which had made the noise on the tiles.

I reached out, caught her by the wrist and drew her into the room.

"Richard!" she exclaimed. "You're free!"

"For the moment," I said, grimly. I led her through the tall windows and on to the terrace. Leaning against the stone balustrade I pulled her down to sit beside me. The stone was warm from the sun; the *cigales* clacked about us. "Just what are you doing here?" I asked her.

"I came to see what they had done to you, Richard. I couldn't bear the thought of what might happen——"

"Your solicitude becomes you——"

"Richard, where is Shelby? Be careful. He's a killer."

"It's a little late to warn me. Shelby and his left-half-section, Gaston are, I hope, securely tied to chairs along the passage. To coin a phrase, my dear, we are alone. Quite incidentally, in case any other friend of yours should happen along, I've got Shelby's gun." I thought I saw something flicker in her eyes as I finished speaking. It might have been fear, but I didn't think so for lack of courage had never been one of her failings. Besides, she had too much confidence in her own attractions ever to be afraid of me.

"What are you going to do?"

"I'm going to turn in my car, if I can find it. I think, since you are here, it would be as well if you came along."

She smiled demurely and I could have smacked her.

"Quite like old times, Richard dear," she said.

There was a big open shed on the left of the courtyard which they evidently used as a garage. This had been outside my range of vision from the window. Someone had run the Jaguar in there.

They hadn't even bothered to take the key out of the ignition. The Luger was lying on the seat where Gaston had tossed it. Well, if nobody wanted it, I did. It was the gun I had used in the war and I liked it. I knew its defects, but I liked it. I put it in my pocket. I was beginning to acquire an armoury.

The Jaguar started first touch and I backed her out into the courtyard.

Of the numberless ways out of the maze of tracks in the Maures I knew three. I could get myself to the road which led over the hills to Le Muy or, in the opposite direction, to the road to Roquebrune, or I could return the way by which I had come.

I decided on the last alternative. It was the shortest route so, in terms of time at any rate, I was less likely to meet Alakov on his way back. And, by taking that way, I should reach more quickly the Corniche and civilization, where it would be all the more difficult to take a shot at me.

As we left the courtyard I threw Shelby's gun into

the underbrush. I wouldn't need it again. Neither would he.

I made the best of my way down the tracks to the coast. I didn't speak while I was doing it for it was too much of a business holding the big car on the rutted, twisting road. I knew I hadn't a hope if I met Alakov and a car full of thugs on their way up. Since the width of the track was barely enough for one car, the only way round was over the edge. Alakov must be due back any time now and it was a toss-up which road he took.

Whether Jacquie knew or was thinking any of this I could not tell. She sat beside me without speaking so I expect that she was. When I saw the beginning of the mat of tarmac which marked where the road ran down to the coast I heaved a sigh of relief. I was never more glad to get back to the everyday perils of driving on the Corniche.

Now it was early evening and the sea had turned that deep, improbable sapphire only to be seen on the coast. The air, too, had that brittle clarity as if it had come through a filter. The buildings looked even more bleached than ever, the colours more stark. With that relaxed feeling of relief which comes after danger past I lifted my foot and let the car run on at forty, the exhaust burbling contentedly behind us.

At Saint-Raphael I had to make my first decision. I had come the shorter road from Cannes over the hills to Fréjus. It seemed better to stick to the more populous coast road on my return. Evening was coming on and I was driving a particularly distinctive car. For all I knew Alakov was back and the alarm was out. A crash in the mountains was easily arranged and was no novelty. A lorry or two went over the side each week in high summer. I also told myself that I should not be hanging about day-dreaming. I took the car fairly fast into Saint-Raphael.

A traffic policeman held us up by the port. As we waited for the line of cars to move on Jacquie spoke for the first time. "What will you do", she said, "if I scream or make to get out or call for his help?"

I had thought of this. I was a jump ahead of her here at any rate. If I tried to frighten her into staying where she was or to threaten her she might well get up to some tricks just for the hell of it.

"It would be easier", I said, "to tell him I haven't got my *permis de voiture*. He'd have to do something about that." I was watching his white-gloved hand. I wished he'd drop it. You never knew with Jacquie; she was unpredictable. I turned and looked at her. She was lying back against the corner where the squab met the car, as elegant as ever, her long, slim legs stretched down the tunnel underneath the bulkhead. Her eyes met mine and I laughed. "Anyway, you're too anxious to see what happens at the end of the road, aren't you?"

Her eyes started to dance. No one ever said that Jacquie was not a damned attractive woman. "Have you grown so interesting, then, little Richard, since last we met?" she said.

The *agent's* baton flicked. I let in the clutch. We were through. I pelted down by the port in third, round the Casino in a rising crescendo and cut out along the promenade to the Corniche and Cannes.

There was a good deal of traffic between Cannes and Nice, and I had to take it pretty steady. I was sweating a bit when we came into Nice. We had been over two hours on the road and the alarm must be out by now.

I found a gap in a line of parked cars well out along the Promenade des Anglais. When I had run the Jaguar into it I got out and took my bag out of the back. "Come on," I said to Jacquie, opening the door for her and tucking her arm affectionately into mine. We climbed on to a bus and I took two tickets to the Place Masséna.

"This is exciting," Jacquie commented. "Now I know what innocent girls feel like when they are being swept off to Buenos Aires."

"If you do it's the only time since you were weaned that you've felt like an innocent girl," I said.

I suppose it was stupid but when we got off the bus and were crossing the Place Masséna I felt every bit as naked and exposed as I used to feel in a bad air-raid. Although I had ditched the Jaguar, Jacquie beside me seemed every bit as flamboyant and distinctive.

The hotel I was making for was off the Rue de France and it was a relief when we got to it. It had been first rate once—about fifty years ago—and it still had the mixture of contemporary and Second Empire décor fashionable at that time. There were open-work gilded lifts, double opening salon doors and cherubims who wanted their bottoms smacked. But it was clean and comfortable and I knew the management.

We got communicating rooms with a bathroom between.

I put my bag on a chair and reached for the telephone. I had to think hard and quickly how to play this out. As I was lifting the receiver a slight noise behind me made me turn. She was in the room, looking at me.

"What is this, Richard?" she said quietly. "Dream fulfilment?"

"Perhaps. Or it might be just self-preservation."

"It might. But is it, I wonder?" She smiled slowly as she said this. "Why didn't you just tie me up with the others?"

"Perhaps you don't appreciate your value as a hostage?"

"I do, indeed. But I don't believe that is the true reason you've brought me along. You're still in love with me, I think, Richard."

That was what I wanted her to think. I knew well her self-confidence, the feeling of power her successes had given her, and, not least, her vanity. She would never believe that the love which a callow boy had once had for her was not still there. And the damnable thing was that she was partly right.

I looked at her framed against the light from the

open window, the fading sun at her back. She was cool, serene and self-possessed. Our eyes met. I knew that she was quite deliberately calling back old times, that she was willing me to remember. And she was succeeding. All at once I could think of nothing but of her and myself together and alone, and that the soft velvety southern night was coming down around us.

Suddenly I was walking towards her. She laughed a little and took my hand and looked up at me. "Not yet, Richard," she said softly. "We have had a long day. We deserve better than this, you and I." She went into the bathroom and I heard the taps running. "Order me a drink," she called. "You know what I like."

It gave me time to pull myself together. For a full minute I stood with my hand on the telephone, thinking. Then I lifted the receiver and told them to send up two bottles of Louis Roederer, a bottle of Bisquit Du bouché, oranges, bitters and lump sugar. After that I got through to the manager's office. He was there and, with my eye on the bathroom door, I spoke to him softly for a few moments. Some sense was coming back to me.

I could hear her humming as I mixed the drinks. Then, with one in each hand I went into the bathroom. "Mmm," she said, as she tasted it. "You have not forgotten the art, Richard."

"I've perfected it. I've had some years to do it in. But no one so nice to drink them with." I played idly with her toes.

"Stop it, Richard, stop it. I'll spill the drink. It's too good to spill. Now—look."

"I'll mix another." I took up the glass. "And hurry up with the tub. Knocking gunmen about and playing Young Lochinvar in this heat makes me need a bath, too."

"Young Lochinvar—who was he?"

I paused in the act of slicing an orange. "He was gallant in love and dauntless in war, but he was a bit slow off the mark. He only got there when she was about to marry another chap."

There was a titter from the bathroom. "Not unlike you, Richard."

" 'The bride kissed the goblet,' " I said. " 'The knight took it up. He quaffed off the wine and he threw down the cup.' " I finished my drink. " 'He took her soft hand ere her mother could bar——' "

"That's *not* my soft hand, Richard."

"No, and your mother isn't here."

"That's just as well. Richard!"

Later we had supper on the balcony. We had *foie gras* rich and creamy, *coq au vin* and *haricots verts*. We finished the Roederer and most of the Bisquit.

We talked. We talked of times past.

"Old friends, after all, are best," I said, sipping my brandy.

"All things old are best, Richard—old friends, old furniture, old gold, old jewels——"

"But not old girls."

"No, not old girls," she laughed. "I hope I shall never be an old girl."

"You'd look pretty quaint with a hockey stick I must say. Old friends, Jacquie," I said again. "About ours, this time. Where is Rupert?"

"Why do you search for him still?"

"My youth or most of it is in Rupert's keeping. It's all bound up with that. You know how I hero-worshipped him. You jibed me about it before. You left me for him. I know that happens to everyone or nearly everyone sometime or other and the sooner the better. I'm older and I know that now. But just the same I want to know the truth about him. Is he a traitor? Is there any explanation?"

"None. And you do know it, Richard. It's no use trying to deceive yourself. He tried to kill you, didn't he?"

"Did he? I've always thought so. But I'd like to hear him say it face to face."

"If you ever find him, he will. He's ruthless. He meant to kill you. He'd do it again." She stretched out her hand to me. "Go home, Richard. Now. Go. It's your last chance. If you don't you will be dead."

"Give me ten minutes with Rupert and I'll go."

"No. I can't."

"Why did Rupert write that book?"

She shrugged. "Poor Rupert. It's one of his weaknesses. He wants to tell people what a splendid chap he was."

"Is that all?"

"Yes. That's all. Don't you know? Didn't you read it?"

"I hadn't time to read the damn thing." The moment I said it I knew that I'd made a mistake. I'd had too much to drink and there was no doubt about it, whatever you thought about her, she was heady company. Before, there might have been some slight suspicion in their minds that I might have learnt something from the book. Now they could gun me down without hesitation anywhere.

"Didn't you, Richard, silly boy," she said, smiling.

She stretched her hand towards me across the table. The long, slim fingers locked in mine. I knew she wanted to reassert her hold over me, to prove to herself that I was still hers to command.

There was only the narrow width of the table between us. She had never looked lovelier. The scent of her hair was all about me as she leant forward. Perhaps she was right. Perhaps I did love her still.

"Lochinvar," she said softly.

Six

RUPERT REDIVIVUS

I slept late and awoke with a throbbing head and the immediate realization that something was wrong. Throwing aside the covers I went through the bathroom into the inner room. It was empty. The door was unlocked. The shutters were open and in the morning sun the speckled Second Empire décor looked tawdry and desolate. There was no note. Nothing. She was gone. Either she had joined her friends or they had found her. Whichever it was I was in deadly peril.

Back in my room I took up the telephone with one hand and jerked the pillow aside with the other. The Luger was still there anyway. That was something.

"I thought I told you to keep an eye on 169 and to tell me if she tried to leave," I barked at the manager.

"*Oui*, M'sieu. It was done. She has not left."

"Hasn't she? The door is unlocked and the room is empty. I don't know what else that means——"

"But, M'sieu Graham, I assure you——"

"All right. Save it. I'm getting out and quick. I'll settle the next time I'm here. Clear me with the desk."

I didn't wait to shave. I slung my things into my bag, stuck the Luger into the belt of my trousers and bolted. I didn't take the lift. I ran down the stairs.

The reception hall of the hotel was L shaped. There was a jewellery showcase at the corner of the L. There some instinct made me pause. Putting down my bag I lighted a cigarette, covering my face with my hands as I did so, and glanced casually round the case. Sitting at a small table, half-hidden, with a packet of Caporal and a glass of Dubonnet in front of him, was Paul Morel.

I drew back quickly, turned round and retraced my steps down the hall. There was another way out through the bar. The bar was empty and in a moment I was standing in the street in the morning sun.

It was almost certain that I would be followed. It was possible that someone would take a shot at me. I had to chance that. Making my way along the Rue de France I came to the Place Masséna and went into a department store. I got to the lift just as it was shutting and went up, alone. I wasn't followed here, anyway.

In the men's section I bought a pair of very brief French shorts, a striped jersey, a loose check jacket, a sailor hat and a pair of smoked glasses. Then I went to the lavatory and put them on. When I came out I glanced at myself in the nearest looking-glass. I'd have knocked 'em in the Old Kent Road, all right. I scarcely recognized myself. After that I made my way to a barber's and had a shave and a crew-cut. That completed the job.

An hour later I had hired a Renault *Quatre chevaux* and was driving back along the coast to Sainte-Marguerite. All the way out of Nice and on the road to Cannes I kept my eye on the driving mirror. No one picked me up. It looked as if I had got away with it.

I felt pleasantly light-hearted in my new identity. Sitting back I let the little car bumble along and enjoyed all the bright colours of the coast.

At Saint-Raphael I stopped and had a ham omelet and a bottle of Kronenburg, ice-cold. Again nobody displayed the least interest in me or my movements. I lunched on the promenade and through the netting below me the chatter of a group of English playing table tennis came up to me. It was all pleasantly normal and reassuring.

Whether it was the beer or not I don't know, but after lunch my head began to throb again. By the time I reached Sainte-Maxime I was feeling hot and tired and confoundedly sleepy. At Beauvallon I gave up. Pulling the *quatre chevaux* into the side of the road I crossed to the beach. There I lay down and put my sailor hat over my eyes. I made a half-hearted attempt to sort things out in my mind but it wasn't much good and in five minutes I was asleep.

Over an hour later I awoke feeling considerably better but with the taste in my mouth and general dopiness about me which comes from sleeping in the afternoon. Pulling on a pair of bathing trunks I waded out into the sea.

There was the usual light breeze and the water was by no means warm. I put my head under and swam down. It was clear and cool, translucent and refreshing. When I came up I lay on my back looking at the craggy green mass of the Maures which guards the coast from storm and rain. For a long time I lay there in that sheltered bay, sometimes turning to look at Saint-Tropez far out beyond me, sometimes swimming idly about, but mostly floating, letting the water lap me.

Now I was trying to think things out.

As far as I was concerned all I wanted to do was to find Rupert. It was true what I had told Jacquie that he had taken my youth with him. I wanted to know why he had done it. Although in the prison camp I had sworn to kill him when I got out I had almost forgotten that now. But I still wanted to find out why he had become a traitor. I had to find that out. He had been my best friend, he had tried to kill me and he had taken my girl. As I recited these things again to myself something of the old blind anger welled up in me. For a second I wondered if I should give way to it again; if, when I met him face to face, I should go berserk as I had done in the prison camp, and shoot him down.

All along I had been using the book as a means to find out about Rupert. But now it was obvious that the book was a lead to something bigger than my mere private vengeance. And it must be important or they would not want me out of the way so urgently. But still, for the moment, the book could wait. It was Rupert I was after.

It was getting dusk when I ran into Sainte-Marguerite. I knew the little town well. Set in a dip in the coast it was off the main highway, which by-passed it. There was a tiny beach, a little port, a casino, and two or three hotels. Unfortunately for those who liked it, it was just on the point of becoming fashionable.

Turning right at the entrance to the town I passed the Roman Catholic church, went through the market and the Place and pulled up at a *pension* I knew. It was small and clean and out of the way. Foreign tourists neither knew it nor bothered about it. It was as safe a hiding-place as any. The proprietor remembered me and had a room for me.

I left my bag on the bed, had a wash and then went out into the town again. The boule players were at their interminable games where the promenade began and, as usual, an argument was developing. I went past them, walked along under the stunted plane trees which the evening breeze was beginning to rustle and turned to the right into the Rue Saint-Martin.

There was a *bar-dancing* here, a tiny place called La Mirabole which catered for the all-night trade. I wanted a word with the barman.

Four high-backed benches were set against one wall of the room making five separate booths with tables in them; beside them was a piano, and two or three tables. An arched doorway screened by a bead curtain led into the back quarters. I never found out for certain what went on behind the doorway, though I could guess.

At the left of the entrance was a small, semicircular bar. I sat on one of the high stools. There was no one else in the place; there seldom was at that time of night.

The barman was bending over a glass in his hands, polishing it with a cloth. He looked up as I sat down. A tiny man with a suspicion of a hunchback he wore uplifts on his shoes to enable him to work at the bar. He had black hair and a jutting nose and eyes that had seen too much too soon.

"Good evening, Mr. Graham," he said.

"Good evening, Herbert. A 'Dry', please."

He busied himself for a few moments behind the bar and then put the drink in front of me. Herbert's dry martinis were served in a glass which came somewhere between a champagne glass and a whisky goblet. They were as pale as ice, as cold as the North Pole and kicked like a Boyes rifle. I sipped mine with respect.

Herbert had been born of one of those crashingly lunatic marriages typical of a certain stratum of life in the twenties. This one had been between a girl from Arkansas who had played the lead in one or two films and an alcoholic Scottish peer. The girl's claims to notoriety were based much more firmly on her private life than on her acting abilities; the peer was about to go bankrupt for the fourth time. They had met, it was said, one wild night in the old Latitude 43 and were married three days later. Then they had set up house in a fantastic Moorish palace in the hills above Collo-briéres which had been built at the whim of a maha-rajah of one of the independent states and never lived in. There Herbert had been born—and left.

The marriage had gone the way of such marriages. His mother jumped out of a hotel window in the crash of '29; the peer came back to live in the place for a year or two before the drink caught up with him and he died in hospital in Nice.

Herbert was left with the walls of the mad palace crumbling about him, the roof falling in, the furniture rotting and the gardens and terraces turning to a wilderness. The peasants had fed him and cared for him and brought him up as best they could. At fifteen he had disappeared into the stews of Saint-Tropez. During the war, when the Germans cleaned up the town, he had escaped and served with the Maquis. He had served them well for he knew every inch of the hills and everyone on the coast. That was why I was sitting opposite to him now, sipping one of his martinis.

"I'm looking for someone," I said. I took a 5,000-franc note out of my pocket and put it between us on the counter, under the edge of the glass.

Herbert stared at the note as if he hadn't seen it. "Yes, M'sieu?" he said.

"He is a man I served with during the war. I have been told that he lives in a villa near here."

"On the coast or in the hills?"

"I don't know. In the hills, I think."

"You set a hard task, M'sieu."

"That is why I come to you."

"He might be anywhere—Saint-Tropez, Ramatuelle, La Croix Valmer, Grimaud—anywhere. What is his name?"

"His name is Rupert Rawle. But that is probably not what he is calling himself now."

Herbert smiled. He had an extraordinary charming smile which lit up his whole face. "What is it that you say, M'sieu—*une épingle*, a pin in a hayfield?"

"A needle in a haystack. You are not far wrong. Look, he walks like this." I got down from the chair and imitated Rupert's walk.

Herbert shook his head. "No, M'sieu, he has not been here. It is difficult."

"I pay well."

"Yes, M'sieu." He had long, thin, aristocratic fingers —those of his father, I supposed. They reached out, flicked up the 5,000-franc note, folded it and tucked it away. I sipped my drink, thinking.

A black Rolls-Bentley slid to a standstill in the street outside the door. A large man in a check sports jacket and a béret came in. He got his bulk on to a stool beside me.

"You speak English?" he asked Herbert truculently. "Yes, M'sieu."

"Good. Double gin and tonic. Got any tonic?"

"Yes, M'sieu." Herbert gave him his drink.

I sat in silence. I had put on my smoked glasses before the man came in. He swallowed his drink in two gulps and ordered another. "Better than this filthy French stuff," he remarked conversationally to Herbert. I assumed, charitably, that he thought I couldn't understand English. "Bit quiet 'ere," he said then.

Herbert leant across the counter and whispered in his ear. All I could hear of what he said was: "Naked women dancing on the tables."

"What!" the big man said. "Later on, eh? Good oh. Be seein' yer." He got down off his stool and went out. The Bentley purred away. My eyes met Herbert's in silent communion. I ordered another drink. I had had time to think while the big man had been in. I resolved to try another approach.

I put a second 5,000-franc note on the counter, remarking to myself as I did so that information was coming expensive tonight.

"There is another," I said. "A friend of the one I am looking for. He is small and squat like a toad. Sometimes he is with a man in a blue blazer and dark glasses."

Herbert glanced up quickly. Then he took up the mixer, poured the martini and put it before me. His face when he looked at me again was impassive. But I knew that I had rung a bell even if, for a moment, I had a horrid fear that it was the wrong one.

"Is he rich?" Herbert asked.

"I think so."

"I do not know but it is like, very like, one who comes here sometimes."

I felt a tingling in my spine. "Yes?" I said.

"He stays late. He drinks a lot but is never drunk. He says that he is M. Isidore, a Swiss industrialist. But I do not think that his name is M. Isidore and I do not think he is a Swiss industrialist."

I sipped my drink. I didn't want to appear too eager. "Why, Herbert?" I asked.

"He asks questions late at night. They are not the questions an industrialist asks. He knows too much about people. He knows too much about me."

Our eyes met. "If he comes in tonight he will not, I trust, know about me," I said. I lifted my hand from another 5,000-franc note. I supposed my life was worth fifteen pounds. The note went the way of the others.

"And where does M. Isidore live?" I asked.

"He has a villa in the hills on the way to Le Muy. It is called Les Cigales. It is on the right-hand side of the road about three miles out. There is a direction post at the entrance to the way which leads to it."

"Thanks," I said.

I finished my drink, paid for it and went out. It was now quite dark. Getting into the *quatre chevaux* I started it up and drove slowly out along the road to Le Muy. Just as Herbert had said, about three miles out a minor road led off to the right. A direction board of the usual type with an arrow-shaped pointer faced me as I drove past it. In the darkness I could not distinguish the lettering.

A few hundred yards farther on I stopped the car and walked back. When I was beside the direction board I could make out the big, blue letters without much trouble. LES CIGALES they said. Up the road a little way was a wooden gate and here a drive began.

Back at the car I took out a large scale map I had bought in Nice and switched on the roof light. There was no difficulty in identifying the turn to Les Cigales. As I had hoped the villa itself was marked and I saw that the woods came down almost on top of it.

If Isidore was Alakov, and my guess was that they were one and the same, it was probable that he took precautions against unauthorized persons blundering about his premises in the night-time. Besides, I had made my preliminary reconnaissance. Tomorrow I could take matters a step further. As I turned the car I debated about going over to Saint-Tropez for dinner. Reluctantly, I decided against it. Too many people were interested in my movements for me to advertise myself. It was probable, I thought, that I had for the moment shaken off Mr. Toad and his minions and it was now more a case of my being after him than he after me. But about Morel I was not so sure.

Morel did know everyone on the coast. That had been no idle boast of his. If I went over to Saint-Tropez, even in my elegant disguise, one of his contacts was almost sure to pick me up. What Morel was after I hadn't the least idea. Perhaps all he wanted was a story for his paper. Perhaps. Whatever it was I had no intention of allowing him to interfere with my plans just now.

Nothing would have suited me better than another martini and dinner on the port, but I put the temptation behind me. Letting the Renault roll down the hill I made my way back to the *pension*.

Not all French cooking is good and I should have remembered that the food at the *pension* was atrocious. I had *soupe aux poissons* which nearly made me vomit, a slice of tough veal and a hard, unripe peach. I tried to make up on cheese and a couple of *fines*, but it wasn't much good. After that I went to bed and had indigestion all night. However, oddly enough, in the morning I felt quite well.

It was another gorgeous day. From my window I could just see one green shoulder of the Maures with a patch of blue sky behind it. The usual faint breeze rustled the leaves of the planes in the streets below. Sounds of children playing came up to me.

After I had had my coffee and *croissants* I washed and shaved. Then I pulled the bedroom table to the window and sat down to write to Saunders. I thought it as well that someone should know what I was doing and how far I had got. Besides, if the book really did mean something, and I guessed that it did, someone besides myself had better know about it. This took most of the morning.

III

When I had finished I got the *quatre chevaux* filled up
with petrol and the tyres checked, posted the letter
and took the road to Le Muy.

Up I climbed into the pines. The road circled and
twisted; below me, as it turned, I could every now and
then see the line of the coast and the blue of the sea.
After climbing for about twenty minutes I reckoned
that I had gone far enough. Pulling the Renault into
a gap in the pine trees I locked it and started to walk.

At first the ground fell away steeply into a small
ravine and climbed just as steeply on the other side.
The trees sheltered me from observation, but also shut
out the breeze. It was hot and I made fairly heavy going. Also, as always happens on these occasions, the
distance was much greater than I had thought.

The ground was broken and where there wasn't a
carpet of pine needles there was a good deal of undergrowth. Altogether I was in a muck sweat when I came
to the edge of the timber. But I had guessed right from
my reading of the map. Les Cigales lay on a ledge of
ground just below where the trees started.

I had come out too far to the left to keep the house
directly under surveillance. Moving along inside the
screen of trees I found a little spur where I had the
front door in my direct line of vision. The twisted cork
oaks grew close together here and I stretched myself out
underneath them. Propping my chin on my hands I
settled myself down to watch and wait.

Facing me was a glass-panelled front door with a

single row of windows on either side. In the right-hand
gable I could see another glass door. This gave on to a
semicircular terrace from which a flight of steps led
downwards. Directly below me was a wide turning-
place for cars.

No sound came from the house. Everything was quite
still. I guessed that the life of the place probably went
on on the other side which faced the coast. There, too,
undoubtedly, was where the main living-rooms were.

Half an hour passed and then an hour and there were
still no signs of life. It was now damnably hot. Moreover, in selecting cork oaks to lie under I had, I
realized, made a bad choice for ants and cork oaks are
inseparable. Very soon I had ants all over me. Amongst
them were those big ones, about the size of one's thumb-
nail. They look terrifying, like something out of a
horror comic, but they don't seem to do more damage
than the ordinary types.

Time went on and still nothing happened except that
I got more and more damnably uncomfortable. I was
beginning to think I would have to make some move
to press home my reconnaissance when, from the far
end of the house I heard the noise of a car starting. A
minute later a pale blue Cadillac came to a standstill
before the front door. A uniformed chauffeur who
looked remarkably like one of the plug-uglies who had
beaten me up in Paris got out of it. Taking a piece of
chamois from somewhere inside the car he commenced
to clean the windscreen in an aimless sort of way.

Suddenly he straightened up and walked quickly round the car. The front door opened and Alakov came out. The plug-ugly whisked open the back door of the car and Alakov got in. He was followed by another thug in a palm beach suit. This man got into the front of the car and I could not see him properly. There seemed something familiar about him, too, but I couldn't place what it was. The chauffeur started the car and they slid off.

By moving my head I could command the road up which I had driven some hours ago. The Cadillac swung on to it and turned in the direction of Le Muy. After about five hundred yards the car went to the left where a little road led into the trees. A flurry of dust marked where it had gone.

Once more I gave my attention to the villa. Silence came down again. I waited for fifteen minutes. Nothing happened. I got to my feet and slid down the bank to the drive. No one took a shot at me. Everything was very quiet. I was suddenly conscious that the clacking of the *cigales* sounded like gunfire in my ears. That meant that I was frightened. I was.

The door had been shut behind Alakov. Bending down I went quickly along underneath the windows to the gable and where the other glass door was. This was open. I stepped inside. My heart was hammering and my breath was beginning to come faster. I took a pull on myself and looked about me.

It was a dining-room running the width of the house.

Opposite me was a french window opening on to a terrace. To my left was a polished door presumably leading to the hallway. The room was furnished with shiny and quite hideous modern furniture. Opening the panelled door an inch I looked out. In front of me was a long hall from which several doors opened. Faintly from the far end of the hall came kitchen noises.

A glance over my shoulder to the front of the house told me that the Cadillac had not returned. Well, I had come to find Rupert, hadn't I? I drew a deep breath and stepped into the hall. Then I went through the villa room by room. There was no one there. I listened to the voices in the kitchen. None of them was Rupert's. I was back in the dining-room when I heard the car returning.

It swept past the window and drew up. It didn't sound like a Cadillac somehow. But I heard Alakov and his bodyguard talking as they came into the hall. Then I heard Alakov speaking into the telephone.

"He knows nothing. You may proceed," he said. There was a pause while I presumed that he was listening to someone on the other end. "Yes," he said. "Yes. The night after tomorrow. She will be here. Eight o'clock." There was a click as he put down the receiver.

I beat it on to the terrace, edging round the corner of the house to see if the coast was clear. The car had gone. I sprinted for the woods. I made them without interference and when I had put a respectable distance between myself and the villa I sat down to think.

Rupert was not at Les Cigales and neither was Jacquie. Moreover, I doubted very much if either of them lived there. But Alakov had gone up that other little road. When he had returned he had spoken into the telephone as if he had seen someone, been talking with him, had verified something. It might well have been Rupert to whom he had been talking. At any rate it was a trail worth trying.

I made my way back to the Renault and drove her up that little road. Like most minor roads in that part of the country it was only the width of a car and the surface was atrocious. Almost immediately after leaving the main road it turned sharply to cross a concrete bridge over a river-bed. Here a thick mass of tall weeds grew; they all but met over the top of the car and shut out the sunlight. Then the road commenced to climb very steeply.

There were numerous dwellings along the way. These were farmers' houses to start with, then, higher up the slopes, were smart-looking summer villas. I remembered Herbert's expression "a pin in a hayfield". It about summed it up.

Then I had an idea. I stopped outside one of the villas and walked in. Near the door a man was busy with a hose, watering a flower-bed.

"I wonder", I said, "if you can tell me in which of these villas a friend of mine, an Englishman, lives. He walks—so." Again I imitated Rupert's horseman's walk.

The man's face lit up immediately in recognition. "Ah," he said. "It is M'sieu Smith. He lives above. The very topmost villa. It is called Les Cascades."

It was as easy as that.

I thanked him and got into the car. The road worsened as we climbed and there were deep, dry, irrigation ditches on either side. I saw Les Cascades, perched on a shelf, surrounded by pines and cork oaks, some time before I got to it. It was white with blue-painted window-frames and doors. Masses of red roses climbed all over it. It looked charming. It would, of course.

I turned the Renault and left her some yards below the house. Then I walked up the sloping ramp to the terrace. Cactus bordered this ramp and the edges of the terrace. Mimosa and almond trees grew about it.

He was sitting in a white wooden lounging chair with blue-and-white striped cushions. There were other similar chairs arranged around a low table. Beside him was a smaller table with drinks on it—Pastis, Gordon's Gin with the buff label, Noilly Prat, bottles of Perrier, an ice thermos. On the table before him was a glass containing Pastis, a delft jug of water and a packet of English cigarettes. Some books were lying about and I saw with amusement that one was Maurice Merevale's latest. Saunders and Renton's imprint certainly got around.

He had aged a little but not much in the years since I had last seen him. His hair was a shade thinner and his face had altogether lost any tendency to youthful indeterminateness and was set forever in its own lines. He had *Le Figaro* in his hands and was glancing at it, but not very attentively, I thought.

I dropped into one of the wooden chairs. The cushions wrapped themselves around my body. Any fatigue I had been feeling seemed suddenly smoothed away. As lounging chairs they were superb. They were, of course, the best that money could buy.

Seven

LE DERNIER COCHON

"Good evening, Mr. Smith," I said. "Or is it Le Colonel Smith? And how is Mrs. Smith?"

"Pretty fit, thanks. I thought you'd show up here sooner or later. What the dickens have you done to your hair?"

"It's commonly called a crew cut. It's my disguise."

"I see. You look as if you were off to Henley to row in the Yale boat."

"Not rowing. Racing and reading were my ploys as you may recollect. You're a writer yourself now, I hear."

I saw him looking at me, openly mocking, in the way I well remembered, the way he had used when I had made a mess of a race or a job he had set me.

"I thought Old England needed waking up," he said. "So from my eyrie overlooking the Mediterranean Sea I blew her a bugle call to arms."

"Indeed."

"We scuttle here, we scuttle there. Wogs kick us in the pants and we hand them over half a country. Chaps write best-sellers about the ability to govern being a mental disease. What, I asked myself, would Sergeant Whatsisname have said about all that? So I said it."

"I should have thought something on the lines of *The Meaning of Treason* better suited to your sterling qualities."

"*Touché*," he said. "What did your publisher friend think of the book?"

So they had their tabs on Saunders. Maybe he would find himself in the middle of a Maurice Merevale plot after all. But it was up to me to keep him out of it if I could.

"He didn't read it," I said.

"That doesn't surprise me. He's an ass."

I experienced the mild shock one gets when hearing an adverse opinion of a friend. "He's a damn good publisher," I said.

"He's an unamiable eccentric who eats men's brains —including yours."

"That's what your intelligence tells you, I suppose. It seems they have me docketed, too. 'A moderately successful amateur rider,' was what Alakov said."

He chuckled. "But how accurate," he said. "I hadn't realized they were as good as that. I still read the racing in *The Times*. You haven't improved much, have you? You're a nice horseman, Richard, and you were anxious to learn. That's something to start on, but it's not enough. You'll never get to the top and I expect you've realized it by now. There are two things necessary to make a top-class steeplechase rider—especially if he's an amateur. You've got to have something which is either born in you or it isn't, and no one knows exactly what it is, and you've got to be more than a bit of a four-letter man. Come to think of it I suppose that goes for success in any walk of life—especially about being a four-letter man."

"You ought to know. You speak from experience."

He laughed again. Then he reached for the bottle of Pastis and tipped some into his glass. Lifting the jug from the table he poured in water and watched the cloud climb in the liquid. "Care for a drink?" he asked.

"No, thanks." This was the second he had had in ten minutes. I wondered if he was drinking too much. If so he didn't show it. The flesh on his face was firm and strong and tanned. As far as I could see he had no-where run to fat. And he was completely at his ease, not a bit discomposed at my appearance. In fact he was in charge of the situation and the conversation as, in my heart, I had always known that he would be.

I was the man who should be calling the odds. I had come on him unawares; I had a grievance, hate, per-haps murder in my heart. And I knew that I could do nothing to him. The old feeling of inferiority had come back and had me by the throat, the old charm had bewitched me again. I knew that man for man he was still my superior. Although I had a gun and I didn't suppose he had, he could have taken me in two minutes.

And I knew that he knew that, too. He sat, sipping his drink, six feet away from me, quite unaffected.

"I don't suppose you've really come here to discuss books, or crew cuts or steeplechase riding," he said.

"I'm not sure why I came. Perhaps I came to kill you."

"An excellent idea. But others have had it and I'm still here."

"All right, you swine, why did you shoot me that night at Callière?"

"You knew too much. I had to put you out of the way."

"Why didn't you do the job properly and kill me?"

"We all make mistakes. You moved at the wrong moment. Things were happening rather quickly just then, if you remember. I hadn't time to go back and finish you off."

I felt as if someone had kicked me viciously in the stomach.

"Then it's true," I said. "There is no explanation. You've been a traitor throughout."

"Correct, my young friend, quite correct."

"Why did you take Jacquie with you?"

For a second his expression changed. "So I took Jacquie with me," he said slowly. Then he smiled again. "I took her because I wanted her," he said. "I've always got what I wanted—surely you remember that. Besides, she was out of your class, Richard. You were never much of a one for going a gallop with the girls, were you?"

"Perhaps not. I did, however, happen to be in love with her."

"She'd have been bored with you in ten days. 'Kind to their women, indeed too kind, no wonder their women go out of their mind.' Who said that?"

"Auden in one of his earlier efforts."

"Never heard of him."

"You may have heard me quote it long ago. So she hasn't tired of you?"

Again some indefinable expression crossed his face. He put the empty glass down on the table with a thump and refilled it. "No," he said. "No. She has not tired of me. Nor I of her, Richard, nor of woman's infinite variety."

"Nor of your splendid life here?"

"No. Why should I? Only millionaires and myself can live as I do on this sheltered coast."

"So you gave up everything you lived for—riding, the cheers of the crowd, your name in the papers, the lights of London, your pick of the racing fillies. . . ."

"Let's face it, I couldn't have stayed on the top much longer. I was getting a bit past it. In a year or so I'd have been the sort of bore who backs you into a corner at a cocktail party and tells you how he rode round Cheltenham in a seven-pound saddle in twenty-eight."

Darkness had come down on us whilst we had been talking. I looked out over the edge of the terrace to the sheen of the Mediterranean far below and the spangled lights of Sainte-Marguerite glowing like fireflies. To the left and behind us was the dark mass of the Maures. The wind had dropped. All was still.

"So it's all been worth it?" I asked.

"Oh, yes. You should know by now, Richard, that I know what I want and I get it." He chuckled. "*Le dernier cochon*, that's me." He chuckled again. "*Le dernier cochon*—the ultimate four-letter man. Rather a neat translation, don't you think?" He put his glass down. "Perhaps you'd like to drink to that?"

"Why yes, Rupert. I believe I would."

He filled the glasses and pushed one over to me.

"*Le dernier cochon*," I said. I tasted the bitter and invigorating drink and then drained it. "Good-bye, Rupert." I turned on my heel and walked down the path to the car.

"*Au revoir, mon vieux*," his mocking voice followed me. "So you are leaving me to history."

I got into the car and started it, my mind in a turmoil. Somehow, somewhere, an idea was nibbling at me. I couldn't get my thoughts clear enough to grapple with it. I hated Rupert. I should have killed him. I had a gun in my pocket. And the world would be well rid of him and I would have laid a twelve-year-old ghost. Or did I hate him? No, dammit, I didn't. The old spell was there again. Despite all that he had done I could go back now and finish the bottle with him and crack old jokes. Finish the bottle—he would probably do that himself. For he was drinking too much unless he needed it to help him through the interview which was in the highest degree unlikely. He had never had resort to jumping powder when I knew him. Perhaps that meant something, perhaps not.

At one point I had thought that he had been trying to tell me something, but clearly he couldn't have been. If he had had anything to say he could have said it straight out for we had been quite alone. No, he was a thoroughly bad lot without a redeeming feature and it was no good trying to deceive myself that he had ever been anything else. The fact that he looked the same, seemed the same and was the same and that I still liked him had nothing to do with it.

The hell with Rupert. The hell with everything. Tomorrow I would be on my way back to London. I'd go overland this time and take my time. I'd stay in Paris for a week and get tight. Then I'd see George Verschoyle about getting the horses ready as soon as possible. Maybe I'd break my neck on the hard. That wouldn't make much stir. "Moderately Successful Amateur Killed at Uttoxeter." No, I wouldn't even rate that across a column in the sporting press.

I slowed and was about to make the turn on to the concrete bridge when a figure stepped out of the reed-beds. The right-hand door was switched open and a man got into the car and sat on the empty seat beside me.

"Did you find him?" he asked. It was Paul Morel.

"Go to hell," I said.

I turned on to the main road and drove towards Sainte-Marguerite.

"Did you find him?" Morel said again. "Listen, Graham, this is urgent, vital."

I drove down the hill towards the town, steadying the car on the corners. "Is it?" I said. "Urgent for your paper? You're getting no scoop from me. Go to hell, Morel."

"I am not a journalist. I am a member of the *Deuxième Bureau.* Now will you listen to me?"

"No."

"You must listen to me. I tell you it is vital. Where is Rawle?" He reached up and shook me by the shoulder.

"If you do that again we'll probably go over the edge. That mightn't be such a bad idea, either. I don't believe a word you're saying."

I parked the car under the plane trees in the Place. Morel got out. He was hopping from one foot to another in fury. "If you don't tell me I'll have you arrested," he almost shouted.

"Hell of a lot of good that will do you. Go ahead and try." I commenced to walk away. "I am going to have something to eat. You can come along if you like, but you needn't go on trying phoney tricks on me. How did you trace me, by the way?"

"Herbert told me you had been in."

"Of course. I might have guessed."

I went down the few steps beside the bridge and

turned to the right. The little restaurant was no more than a few boards well-scrubbed and laid on the sand, a white-painted wall with pictures in bright colours and five tables with checked cloths on them. It was as neat and gay as I remembered it. The two pretty girls who served in their print dresses were as neat and gay as the place. I had another pastis and ordered my meal. Morel sat opposite to me and glowered.

A rim of the moon had come out of the sea. It was splashing the darkness with silver. I spread terrine and looked at the curve of lights around the bay. Well, I had found Rupert and I wished I hadn't. Whatever had happened to him he had not altered. Unlike Shelby he was still a good man to go tiger shooting with. By and large there was no one I would rather have had beside me. Only now he was beside the tiger. Perhaps we never did alter. Shelby must always have been rotten at the core. But then Rupert must be rotten, too—I gave it up.

Morel was talking again. "Graham, I implore you in your own interests to heed me. I am telling the truth. I *am* from the *Deuxième Bureau*——"

One of the girls put a bottle of *vin blanc* between us. I poured out a glass and pushed it across the table to Morel. "Drink that and stop talking rot," I said.

"Very well. I will give you this one last chance. You can come to La Mirabole with me and ring up London and verify what I say. I can get you through in ten minutes. I know the number you will ring. There is an *agent* at the head of the steps now. I have only to strike my glass twice, thus"—he picked up a knife and rapped it sharply against his glass, making it ring—"and he will come down and you, my friend, will do what ringing you have to do from La Poste. Make your choice."

I began to take him more seriously. The reference to London had an authentic ring about it. Morel's face was hard and set and his eyes were cold. "All right, Morel," I said. "I'll go to La Mirabole with you. You can put through the call since you know the number."

There was an *agent* at the head of the steps. He was lounging against the wall staring out to sea. Of course Morel might have noticed him when we were coming down and used his presence to bolster up his story. Then, again, perhaps not. Perhaps Morel was what he said he was. The telephone call would prove things one way or another in any case.

We got a booth at the back of the restaurant. There were only one or two people there. A man in a Jamaican shirt with one of those moustaches which look as if they have been drawn on with a stick of greasepaint was playing the piano. The English tourist in the béret was at a table beside the dance floor. He had a friend with him now. The friend was a little man in an even louder check coat. He had slicked-back hair and very large hands. The big man glanced at me as we came in. I wondered if he recognized me. It was unlikely and anyway his mind was probably too full of the naked women who were to dance on the tables later on, to bother about anything else. I ordered *fines à l'eau.*

"Well," I said to Morel. "Since you know the number, go ahead."

He went out through the bead curtain. I looked at my drink, rattled the ice in it, sipped it and waited. I thought I might go to Tangier instead of going back overland. I could catch a liner from Gib. when I wanted to return. Or I might fly home via the West Indies and Canada. I'd want to get back in time to ride work before the season started. And I ought to let George Verschoyle know what I was doing. That is, if I really was getting out. . . .

Almost to the second of the tenth minute Morel was back. He jerked his head towards the bead curtain. "The call is through," he said. "The door opposite. Close it before you speak."

The room was furnished, very barely, as an office. There was a rickety wooden filing cabinet, a roll-top desk, a table and some chairs. I picked up the telephone.

"Robinson, metalwork department," the high-pitched voice said. Presumably he never went to sleep.

"Graham here," I said.

"Paul Morel is what he says he is. You may co-operate." There was a click and that was all. Robinson never had been a talkative chap.

I went back to the table. "All right," I said. "I've been a fool. Now what do you want?"

"Did you find Rawle?"

I hesitated, then: "Yes, I found him," I said.

"Ah——" he stopped. Someone was standing beside our table. We both looked up. It was Herbert.

"Gentlemen," he said. "You have everything?"

Morel ordered two more *fines à l'eau.*

"I see our friend of the Bentley is here again," I said to Herbert.

"Last night he came and was disappointed."

"No naked women?"

"No. Tonight, who knows, he may be more fortunate."

I glanced idly across the room. The big man's eyes suddenly shifted. He had been studying us. He said something to his companion, looked at the piano-player, at his drink—and back at me again.

Suddenly I remembered why the purr of the motor which had brought Alakov back to Les Cigales had sounded different. It was the purr of a Bentley. Also I remembered why the second thug at Les Cigales had seemed familiar. I looked hard at the big man, especially at that portion of his coat under his left arm. The bulge was there all right. You wouldn't have noticed it unless you were looking for it, but I was and it was there. All sorts of warning bells jangled in my brain.

Herbert came back with the drinks.

"Your friend," I said. "You are sure he is just what he seems to be—just an English tourist?"

Herbert laughed contemptuously. "Could he be anything else?"

"I see. Then why is he carrying a gun?"

Both Morel and Herbert stiffened.

"Find out—quickly," snapped Morel. Then he turned to me. "Now and then you amaze me by a shaft of intelligence," he said.

Herbert moved quietly across the room. He bent over the table as if to serve them. But they were alerted. They knew they had been rumbled. The big man muttered something to the other. They tensed.

Suddenly everyone was looking at their table. The pianist stopped in the middle of a bar. The atmosphere in the place had become electric.

The big man started to get to his feet. His right arm moved. Herbert brought his tray down, edge first, like a sword, on to his forearm. The big man gave a howl of pain, cursed and swung at Herbert. Morel and I got to our feet.

"Out," Morel hissed at me. "Through the back."

But we weren't quick enough. The little thug was across the dance floor like a striking snake. He was almost on top of me when Morel kicked him in the stomach. Something glittered under my arm and a knife pinned my coat to the woodwork. I pulled free with a tearing of cloth. Morel was through the curtain, holding it back.

Someone, I think it was the pianist, tried to get between me and the door. I shoved the *fine à l'eau*, glass and all, rim uppermost, into his face. "This is getting bloody rough," I said.

Then I was out in the little hallway behind the curtain. Morel threw open the office door. Kicking it shut behind him, he turned the key in the lock. Sounds of battle came from the bar. Morel jumped to the window and threw it open. It was only a drop of a few feet to the street below.

"Run for the car," Morel commanded.

I felt exhilarated, I don't know why. Probably it was the satisfaction of hitting someone. "I don't care much for your friends," I said, as we ran. "That's not the sort of behaviour expected in the Members' enclosure at Sandown."

"Save your breath for making jokes when we are out of trouble," Morel snapped back. "Here is the car. *Monte*—quickly."

The noise of running feet came to us clearly. Someone had shaken free of the fight and was after us.

I put my finger in the starter ring and pulled. The engine fired immediately. I let in the clutch and we shot down the Place.

"Make for the hills," Morel ordered. He was half-turned in his seat, looking out the rear window. "I hope you are satisfied with what you have done," he went on, as we started to climb. "If you'd believed me in the first place this wouldn't have happened."

I was feeling a bit of a fool about this, but I didn't see why I should admit it. "If you had taken me into your confidence instead of masquerading as a journalist, it wouldn't have happened, either," I answered. "What are you after anyway, Morel?"

"I'll tell you as much as you need to know when we get out of this little affair—if we do."

"Aren't we away in a hack?"

"The lights of a car are coming up fast after us from Sainte-Marguerite," he said calmly. "Turn left into the Col de Gratteloup."

I glanced into the mirror. Sure enough there the lights were, two yellow baleful eyes coming hard up the hill and gaining.

It was lucky I knew the roads. "I'll kill the lights," I said. "It's a chance. He might go straight on."

Morel grunted. He was again half-turned in his seat. He reached under his left armpit and an American service automatic appeared in his hand.

"Good God," I said. "Where do you carry all that artillery?"

He did not answer but continued to stare back at the lights. On the bends they sent great shafts over the valley or into the sky. They were getting nearer.

The sharp right-angled turn into the Col came up then. I switched off our lights, changed down and pulled the little car over the bridge and up the steep incline beyond. My foot went hard down and we were round the first hairpin before the car behind came to the cross.

"He's gone straight on, I think," Morel said. "We've got a respite, anyway. Push on."

I was doing all I could and so was the little car. She was a game little brute but I wished I had more engine under me.

The road over the Col de Gratteloup, as anyone who has driven it knows, is nothing but a series of hairpin and semi-hairpin bends hacked out of a pine forest on the side of a hill. I went up it as you might go up a ladder with the bends as steps. I was using the lights again now and was using the whole width of the road too, sliding the bends and making the little engine scream in its top revs in each gear.

As we ran up one of the steep inclines between the bends I heard Morel swear. Risking a glance back I saw his reason. The lights were after us again.

"Can you keep away from him?" Morel asked.

"I'll try, but I doubt it. That's probably the black Bentley I saw before. If that tough knows how to drive, and he probably does, he'll be on top of us in about three minutes."

"Perhaps I'll discourage him," Morel pushed open his window.

"Mind what you are doing with that cannon," I said. "This car isn't mounted to carry it."

The noise when he fired nearly lifted me out of my seat. I don't suppose his shots went within miles of them. At any rate they didn't slow the other driver. Whoever he was he knew what he was doing. He began to close up fast. The lights were almost licking me now as I scudded round the corners.

"If I could get to Le Revest I might be able to slip him again at the cross," I said. "But I'm not going to get there at this rate. Cripes! What was that?"

Something had hit the roof an almighty crack six inches above my head.

"He's making good shooting," Morel commented professionally. He turned inside the car and fired through the rear window three times. What with the noise and the crash of breaking glass I didn't know whether we were being hit or hitting back.

Only the corners were saving us now. The next straight stretch w met we were for it. We would be pinned in the lights like a fly on a wall.

"Get set to jump," I said. "I'm slinging her across the road at the next corner. Ready?"

"O.K."

The door catch was under my left hand. I released it and held the door.

This had to be timed to a second if it were to work. I lifted my foot.

For an instant we were outlined in the lights with the great car behind hurtling down on to us. A fusilade of shots ripped out. One came in through the rear window and smashed into the fascia. It went rattling around inside like a pea in a tin.

I stamped on the brake and swung the wheel hard over. She skidded sideways, her tyres scrabbling, lurched on to two wheels—and settled back.

"Jump!" I shouted.

The door had been wrenched out of my hand. I dived sideways through the opening. The road hit me. It was about as hard as Devon and Exeter in August. I slid along collecting gravel rash, rolled over and stood up.

It worked. I couldn't have timed it better if I'd been practising for weeks. The Bentley hit the back of the Renault with a crash like a giant kicking a tin can. From the far ditch Morel's automatic talked again. Out of control the big car swung to the edge of the road. For a split second it hung there. Then it drove forward, engine roaring, out into space.

The drops from the road in that part of the Maures are not prodigious but thirty feet is a fair distance for a heavy piece of machinery like the Bentley to fall. There was a rending and tearing of trees and branches, and then a dull thud which shook the ground on which we stood.

Morel's voice sounded in my ear: "Come on. Get going. Get into the woods." He was running as he spoke and I followed him. In a minute or two he stopped for breath. We were now quite safe. If anyone got out alive and unhurt from the Bentley they were scarcely likely to be in a condition to pursue us.

Morel, of course, had a pocket compass. He seemed to travel with equipment sufficient for an armoured division. I don't know where he stowed it all. He looked normal enough when you met him.

When we had got our breaths back he laid the compass on his hand and consulted it. Then he took a quick look about him and set off at a sharp pace. I followed him. There was precious little else I could do.

I was still fairly fit from riding but it took me all my time to keep up with him. The going was rough under foot and the ground there is broken up into a series of little valleys. Watercourses, dried up at that season, ran through these. We had to go down to each watercourse, search for and find a way across and then climb up the other side.

After about an hour of this Morel stopped, took another bearing and then swung away at a tangent up a steep incline. It looked to me as if we were climbing into the main mass of the Maures instead of going parallel to them along their slopes. However, he went purposefully as if he knew where he was going. It seemed that he did for some way below the crest we came out on to a road. VIRAGES 4 KM announced a signpost beside us.

"Where are we?" I asked. "Between Le Revest and Plan de La Tour?"

Morel nodded. "Correct," he said. "We will use the road now."

"I hope the *Deuxième Bureau* are going to pay my garage bill."

"I will see. It may be difficult, but I will see," he answered seriously.

"You'll be darn lucky if I don't indent for a Rolls."

"We can talk about that later. Now we must walk."

Soon we were over the top of the Col and dropping down the other side. The moon lit up the whole country-side with its grey radiance. Far below, in flashes, I could see the sea. Nobody was about, there was no traffic on the road. We were quite alone. The road fell steeply through the pines in a succession of curves. Rounding one sharper than most we were all of a sudden in the little village of Plan de La Tour.

Morel went to a house and hammered on the door. After his third knock it opened. I saw a thin and tousled man, his face grey with sleep. There was a rattle of conversation and the door shut again. In a few moments we heard the noise of a motor-car engine starting up. Then round the corner of the house came one of those ancient Citroens with disc wheels and a box body. It was painted rust colour, its lights were merely pale yellow blurs in the darkness, but its engine sounded healthy enough.

Morel pulled open one of the rear doors and we got in. The driver engaged the gear with a crash. We trundled off up the avenue of stunted planes and turned to the left.

"Where now?" I asked Morel.

"La Garde Freinet," he answered. "I want to get you under cover, my friend."

I sat back on the worn upholstery. The rim of a spring dug into my buttocks. We were directly over the rear axle and every bump went straight into us. They were heroes who rode far in old-time motor-cars.

"Before I do that you can tell me what all this is about," I said.

"I will. But first—you found Rawle?"

"I did."

"Where is he?"

"I think I'll know just what you are up to before I tell you that," I said. He gave me a venomous look. I was reminded that I had never really liked him. I didn't know how far I trusted him even now. "If you want my help stop treating me as a half-wit. Come on. Come clean, Morel."

He appeared to make up his mind. "Very well," he said. "It seems I must."

"I take it your boy-friend doesn't speak English." I nodded at the driver.

"He does not and he is too stupid to understand even if he did," Morel said contemptuously.

It occurred to me that two of the Frenchman's characteristics had hardened over the years. One was his intolerance of the ability of anyone but himself, and the other his lack of a sense of humour. Probably the two went together.

He lighted a Caporal, took a deep pull on it and exhaled slowly. Then he began to speak. "Alakov", he said, "is the Director of Soviet espionage for Britain."

"I guessed that."

"You may or may not know that the holder of such a position always lives outside the country which he controls—usually in the one adjoining."

"Yes, I know that."

"At the moment he is on to something big. What it is we are by no means sure. There is, as you may know, an Anglo-American conference commencing in Paris on Monday. Relations between our two splendid countries are by no means as good just at this moment as they might be. The conference amongst other things hopes to iron out points of difference. In fact, it must. The prosperity certainly, possibly the safety of the western world, depends upon it. Now, overtly, Soviet policy is all friendliness these days. But make no mistake about it, their ultimate aims are just the same—the propagation of Communism to bring the world under their domination. Their methods have changed but that is all. In the view of most people who know any-thing about world affairs the present policy of peaceful penetration is much more dangerous than the crude doctrines of Stalinism. Then the danger was so obvious even an effete democracy like yours was alerted to it. Now you will be only too anxious to believe their good intentions because it suits your sloth even as you per-suaded yourselves to shut your eyes to Hitler. This time there will be no second chance."

"You seem quite pleased about it, Morel."

"I do not like the destinies of my country being once more tied to a people who are temperamentally opposed to us and who have already once abandoned us to the Hun."

"That's one way of looking at it. I'm not going to get

into a political argument with you. How does Rupert fit into all this?"

"The Soviet mean to sabotage the conference, if they can. That book has something to do with their plan. We believe it to be in code. But we have utterly failed to break the code."

"Did Rupert write it?"

"We do not know and the point is immaterial anyway. It is a record of his war experiences. It has been accepted for publication by a small firm who recently started business. The firm is, of course, financed by foreign money. The scheme was, we believe, that this firm was to get the book from an agent, a fly-by-night, so that were there any questions to be asked then they could say that they knew nothing of its origin beyond having got it from an agent. As you know there was a bungle. The typescript was sent to Saunders and Renton whose name resembled that of the other firm and thus it came into your hands. It has since been restored to the original publishers."

"Alakov can't call the plan off even though he knows we may have caught on to something?"

"Quite. He daren't confess to his superiors that there has been a bungle or his own head will roll. Who rides a tiger must never dismount. He treated you comparatively leniently at first for the same reason. He hoped to frighten you off and thus avoid any possibility of publicity and a leakage back to his bosses. Now he must get rid of you at all costs."

141

"But what is it all leading to?"

"That is what we do not know and must find out. From information we have received we believe that the key to the code is being brought to England in the near future. How, we do not know. Consider the ways open to them—it might be brought in a passenger's luggage, by an aeroplane landing in a lonely field, by a frogman on a forsaken beach, by any of a thousand ways."

"Quite. It's like looking for a pin in a hayfield."

Morel glanced at me. Then he said precisely: "That is not the right idiom, Graham. You have been speaking French too much. It is then one confuses one's own language. 'A needle in a haystack' is the correct expression."

"So it is. Forgive me, Morel. Why don't you get the official secrets people to close down on the book?"

"Because even the book and key, we are convinced, is not the whole story. As I have said, overt friendliness is now the plan. This is something subtle. Whatever it is it is bound up with Rawle and the girl. He has been kept alive and in luxury for years, and as far as is known nothing has been demanded of him. It is Rawle and the use to which he is being put who alone can supply the answer for which we are looking. This, I am convinced, is where he repays his debt. Now you know why I am so anxious to find him. Where is he?"

"In a villa called Les Cascades above the reed-bed where you got into my car," I answered rather sulkily.

Why, I don't know, but it still went against the grain to split on him.

"You were with him some time. Did he say anything that might help us?"

"We talked of old times. He told me I wasn't enough of a four-letter man to head the amateurs' list. I know what he meant. He hadn't forgotten the idiom."

Morel eyed me suspiciously. "Rawle is a traitor," he said. "He tricked you over a girl and tried to kill you. You tell me you met him and discussed horse-racing and you expect me to believe it. You are puerile, Graham."

"And you'd better start getting more civil. You are darn lucky I don't bat your ears back and sling you out of the car."

"More childishness. And the charming Miss Leroux with whom you spent some time in Nice? You learnt nothing from her?"

"Lots. But nothing to assist you."

"You are not helpful."

"What the hell do you expect? I've told you where to find Rupert. I know no more."

"Will he do what they want? He will, I think. He was always rotted by luxury, Rawle."

"He didn't get three gongs for being rotted by luxury."

Morel smiled to himself and sat back in his corner.

The old Citroen groaned in low gear up the hill into La Garde Freinet. It passed the turn down to the coast and went up the narrow street under the frowning rock.

"I thought you were stopping here. Where are you going?" I asked.

"A place to hide you. You will see."

So we trundled on through the hills. Presently the driver turned to the left on to a narrow path. It was of much the same width and surface as those which climbed and twisted about The Crouching Lion. Pines and cork oaks grew around it on either side and pressed close upon it. We could not go more than walking pace and we banged and bounced over rocks and into holes. This was certainly out of civilization. I looked at Morel sitting silent and grim beside me. For the first time I began to feel uneasy.

"What are you up to, Morel?" I said.

"No one will find you where we are going," he said. "You surely realize, Graham, that your life is forfeit. You have caused Alakov the maximum amount of trouble even to the possibility of putting his own life in danger. You have only to show yourself on the coast for them to kill you."

Hardly had he finished speaking when we came out of the trees on to a small plateau. Below us, about a hundred yards away, lay a range of ruined buildings. They stood out stark and white in the moonlight like the bones of a skeleton. To the left of them an immense roofless church towered over the lot.

The car bumped forward over the rough surface of

the plateau. The driver turned on to a path which ran along beside the ruin and came to a standstill in front of a broken cloister.

"We have arrived," Morel said.

The cloister was high and vaulted. There were gaps in its roof through which one could see the sky. We walked down it, our feet ringing on the flags. At intervals we passed black, gaping doorways leading, I supposed, into monastic cells. An archway brought us into a smaller cloister. Here the trickle and bubble of flowing water came to my ears.

Morel turned to the right. After a few steps he stopped and pulled open a door in the wall. It came towards us slowly, its hinges protesting, as if it had not been used for a long time. Morel went in and beckoned to me to follow.

A match flared and I saw Morel bending over a pressure lamp. In a few moments it spurted into light and I could take stock of where we were.

It was a fair-sized chamber with walls of rough stone. There was a covered roof and an earthen floor. In the centre was a great stone slab which might have been a primitive table or a tomb. Round the walls, about three feet from the ground, ran a stone shelf.

As I looked about me I became aware of another fact. The driver had followed us in and was standing near the door.

"L'Abbaye de Calumet," Morel said, blowing out a match. "We used it extensively during the war and it is kept stocked for emergencies like this one. I hope you will find it comfortable, Graham."

"I don't much care for the look of it," I said. "How long am I supposed to hole up here?"

"Until I have finished what I have to do. I will leave instructions that you will be provisioned."

"How am I supposed to spend my time? Counting rats? This place reeks of them."

"Your great leader Winston Churchill when he was on the run in South Africa said he became quite friendly with the rats. I suggest you cultivate the same taste."

"No dice, Morel," I said. "Find somewhere better for me to sleep. Another of our great leaders, Lord Roberts, V.C., was allergic to cats. I'm the same way about rats and I don't intend to spend a week cooped up with a whole colony of 'em. Come on, back to the car."

All of a sudden the big automatic was in his hand. "I'm afraid you are staying here, Graham, whether you like it or not."

"What the devil do you mean?"

"I don't trust you to co-operate with me. You can't expect me to believe the story that you talked horse-racing with Rawle for half an hour. You know more than you have seen fit to tell me. You and Rawle and Miss Leroux were very friendly once. Who knows, you might find old ties once more too strong were I to set you at liberty."

"You have a nice way of repaying those who help

you. But here's a tip, Morel. Don't try to take Rupert by yourself. Call in the Foreign Legion and you might have a chance."

"Just as I thought. Still the hero-worshipper. The English have always preferred personal liking to impersonal honour. Goering was such a good chap, wasn't he? He might almost have been to a good public school. You're typical of your type, Graham. No wonder you're a dying race. The rats won't be the only vermin round here."

"Why, you . . ." I took a step towards him.

It was the driver, of course. If I hadn't been so fogged with sleep and so furious at that last crack I might not have walked into it so easily. I saw Morel look over my shoulder and give a faint nod. I tried to turn but it was too late. Something seemed to explode in my head. Some interesting specimens of fireworks in silver and orange flashed in front of my eyes. Then a cloud pushed by a trip-hammer came down on top of me. That was all for a bit.

Eight

L'ABBAYE DE CALUMET

When I came to I had a splitting headache. At first I thought that I had been out on some immortal binge and was waking with a hangover. Then, when I found my face pressing into a damp, earthen floor, memory began to come back to me. I moved my head. Pains shot through it, but I could move it. My limbs worked, too. I opened my eyes.

A large, black rat was sitting five yards from my face looking directly at me through his tiny, evil eyes.

"Christ!" I said, and jumped to my feet. A stab of pure pain, like two electric wires meeting, shot across my temples. The rat turned and made for the side of the room at an unhurried lope. There was nothing to throw at him to help him on his way. My knees felt as if they were about to give way and I sat heavily down on the stone slab in the middle of the room. The rat paused and looked over his shoulder, then he slid quietly into a hole in the wall.

Sunlight was coming through a small, rectangular

window high up in the massive outer wall. The pressure lamp had gone out but the room was bright enough. My watch had not stopped. A glance at it told me that the time was twelve o'clock.

The door was made of some heavy wood and looked solid. An inspection showed that it was securely locked. The window was far above my reach and in any event was too narrow to allow me to pass through it. The whole room smelt of dampness and disuse and my head was throbbing like hell. I could hear rats at work in the walls—whole regiments of them, it seemed. There was a small hole in the masonry opposite to me, underneath the shelf. A rat put his nose to this, looked about him, and withdrew.

I shivered. What I had said to Morel was no exaggeration. I am terrified of rats. Always I had consoled myself for this illogical and, I suppose, despicable weakness, with the thought that the late Lord Roberts had been terrified of cats. But that wasn't going to do me much good now. I felt that I might be sick at any moment. I also felt that I should go mad if I had to spend another night in this horrible chamber.

At that moment I put my hand into the pocket of my coat and found that I was touching the Luger. It isn't possible, I thought. But it was there, all right. Just to make sure I took it out and looked at it. There it was, cold and heavy on my hand. What is more it was still loaded and the spare clip was in my other pocket.

Hefting it in my hand, the feel of its worn butt bringing manhood back to me, I tried to make myself think. Had Morel left the gun there for a purpose or had he slipped up? If he had left it there for a purpose I could not even begin to think what it was. But with all his confidence in his brains and with all his vaunted efficiency he still could make a mistake. His must have been tired last evening and his mind was full of his plans and his problems. He didn't know that I had a gun for I had not used it. It was probable that he had had me slugged and left me. Or was it? At any rate it was as good an assumption as another and the one I intended to work on. I stepped up to the door and blew the lock off.

My first instinct was to burst out into light, fresh air and freedom. But I fought it down. If Morel had left a gaoler he would come immediately to investigate the shots. I had better be ready for him if he did. If it was the driver I would be glad to meet him. He might not, however, be so pleased to meet me, especially now that I had a gun in my hand.

Placing my back to the wall beside the door I waited. Ten minutes exactly by my watch I stayed there pressed against the wall. Two rats came out and hopped about. I almost broke and ran, but I held on to myself and stuck it out. No one came. I walked into the free air outside.

It was the smaller of the two cloisters in which I found myself. With its rounded, Romanesque arches and narrow pillars it must have been charming once. Now it was broken and desolate and, like the room in which I had been imprisoned, the smell of decay was upon it. There were gaps in the masonry, most of the surrounding buildings had fallen in and the court which it enclosed was thick with tangled grass and weeds. Two small cypresses which grew there seemed somehow to enhance the churchyard air of desolation.

The sound of water which I had heard last night came from a spring in the centre of the court. There had once been a fountain there but now the stone bowl and its pedestal lay forlornly amongst the weeds. The water ran away through a stone watercourse and into a pipe on the far side of the cloister.

For a few more moments I stood in the silence, waiting. I heard no sound but the gurgle of the spring. Then I walked across to it. Stepping over the broken pedestal I knelt down. Like one of Gideon's men, with the Luger still in my hand, I put my head into the cool dark pool and drank.

When I had quenched my thirst and washed myself as best I could I stood up and looked about me.

The way we had come last night was behind me. I went back under the archway into the bigger cloister. Only one side of this, I saw now, still stood. Where the rest had been was an open space with one or two fragments of masonry marking the old walls. Beyond these was the plateau we had crossed in the Citroen and, two hundred yards away, bordering it like a curtain, the forest.

There was nothing much to be seen here so I turned and retraced my steps, went through the smaller cloister and entered the great church. It was roofless; vast, echoing and empty. Smooth walls of biscuit-coloured stone soared upwards to end in jagged broken pinnacles outlined against the sky. The stillness was almost terrifying. I found myself wanting to run, ready to do anything to get out of the place.

Opposite where I was another arched doorway appeared to lead to the back of the whole range of buildings. I walked towards it, past where the high altar must once have stood, through a line of great rounded pillars towering upwards, and entered this doorway.

A short, vaulted passage suddenly ended in a jumbled mass of fallen stones. Climbing these I found myself in the open again, this time behind the buildings.

The ground fell away steeply in front of me. Then it climbed to a ridge. Over this ridge rose another, higher and longer, which cut across the skyline. This higher ridge was heavily wooded, but I thought I could make out the zigzag scar of a road climbing up it. I resolved to make for this road.

Nearby the ground was like the plateau in front, bare and open. The valley into which I descended was dark and overcast, surrounded on all sides by great crags and outcrops of rock. There were white, splintered stumps of dead trees sticking up here and there like broken bones. Although the sun was blazing, in the valley the air felt dank and cold. Behind and above me was the huge range of broken buildings of the abbey. Sightless windows stared down at me like the eye-sockets of a skull. I had the feeling that I was being watched, brooded over, and threatened. The farther down into the valley I got the more dank and chill became the air.

At the very bottom was a stream. Unlike most streams in those hills it had not dried up nor disappeared for the summer months. It was just too wide to jump. Dark and opaque it was in keeping with the rest of the horrible place. I plunged into it and the cold ate at me. The water came up to my waist as I waded across. I had a horrible feeling that I was going to have to swim and that I would not be able to, that I would be sucked down to drown in that dank and evil stream. Then I had hold of a branch and was pulling myself out.

Immediately I started to climb the other side of the valley. The going was fairly good for which I was profoundly thankful for my one wish just then was to get out of the place and away from the brooding presence of the abbey.

I do not know nor have I ever tried to find out what secrets that abbey and its valley held but if ever I felt evil I felt it there. No birds flew or sang in the valley; there was no life of any sort. Not even a lizard slid away from me as I walked. Everything shunned the place.

When I reached the top of the crest I could see over into a more pleasant, wooded landscape. Moreover, I had been right. A road did climb up the far shoulder. I could now clearly see its mark as it cut through the trees. At a guess I put Collobrières below me and to my right. Before this I had only been impelled by my urge to get away from the abbey, but now I realized that I must decide where I was going.

If I was right then the road which I could see led into the Fôret Dominiale du Dom, across the main road from Cogolin to Hyères and thus over the hills to Bormes and Le Lavandou. To verify my guess I decided to make for it. Once I knew definitely where I was I could plan my further movements.

Before I left them something made me turn to look for the last time at the valley with the abbey, bare, bleached and sinister, lying at its lip. As I looked I thought I saw a movement at the doorway from which I had left the buildings. The movement, if movement it was, was only the slightest thing. Probably I should not have noticed it at all had not my nerves been stretched so tight. Under the shade of a rocky outcrop I waited, watching, my eyes fixed on the spot. The movement was not repeated. Dismissing it as a trick of eyesight or possibly a shifting of the stones and rubble collected there, I went over the crest and began to make my way down through the woods.

It took me two hours' hard walking in the heat to get on to the road and another hour to get to the top of the Col. When I did so I found that my recollections of the ground had not failed me and that my guess as to my whereabouts had been right. From a lay-by built out of the hillside at the very top of the Col I could see the outlines of the Presqu'île de Giens and beyond it, slumbering in the heat, the Isle d'Hyères. I was on the Col de Babaou and I was in command of the situation in that I knew where I was and where I could go.

The immediate point to be thought out was what I was going to do. After what Morel had told me it was clear that I could not give up now. Whatever use Rupert was going to be put to it was obvious that it was something which vitally affected the interests of my country, something which it was up to me to stop if I could. Moreover, there were still lingering doubts in my mind now that I had put twenty-four hours between myself and that interview with Rupert, and the first impact of it had worn off. If Morel had not been so sure of himself and his own cleverness and so unsure of me I would have told him of my thoughts and guesses. Now I would have to do it all by myself. Perhaps it was better that way. Perhaps only I could do it. Rupert, Morel had said, was the heart of the plan. I must find him again, find out from him what was being demanded of him and, most vital of all, find out if he was going to do what his masters wanted. If he was then I must stop him.

Morel had said that I was a marked man and he was probably right. Obviously Sainte-Marguerite was going to be a highly dangerous place for me to set foot in. But I had to get there just the same.

Eight o'clock, Alakov had said in his telephone conversation. I was as sure as I could be of anything that he was confirming the deadline. I looked at my watch. It was now close on six-thirty. I had, as near as made no matter, just twenty-four hours.

How far Alakov's hand could reach was a matter of conjecture. No doubt he did have agents all along the coast but they could hardly check on every tourist. I resolved to come in by the back door, as it were. I would make the best of my way to Le Lavandou, there change my identity as best I could and get one of the local buses to Saint-Tropez. From Saint-Tropez it should not be impossible to make an approach to Sainte-Marguerite by sea. It was the point from which they would least expect me.

I got up from the bench on which I was sitting and made my way down the Col.

Soon the sun began to drop and the air became cool. I had eaten nothing all day and I was desperately tired. My head was throbbing again and there was a large tender lump on the back of it. I kept on going until the sun dropped out of the sky like a stone going into the water. There wasn't much point pressing on in darkness. Besides, I was just about all in.

While there was still enough light I turned off the

road and looked for a place to sleep. Whatever I found would be better than dossing down with the rats. Choosing a spot where the carpet of pine needles seemed thicker than most I stretched out on them. I think I was asleep as soon as I closed my eyes.

Nine

LOVE TROUBLE

When I awoke the sun was well up. It was extraordinarily peaceful in the forest in the hills. The quiet could almost be felt. Above, the sky was blue and unclouded. The air was sweet with the scent of pines. A pleasant lassitude possessed me. I felt I could stay on there forever.

Propped up against a tree, relaxed and only half awake I did, in fact, lie on letting time go past me. The pine needles were soft and I had got used to the ants or the ants had got used to me. Hunger and exhaustion produce the feeling of living on another plane somewhere between this world and the next, and both of them were having their way with me. No urgent sense of purpose now possessed me as it should have done and had done last night. Closing my eyes I let the faint, fragrant, breeze from the sea come up and caress me. This was better than being chased all over Provence by angry men. To hell with everything. I began to doze off again.

It was the sound of voices that roused me a second time. At first I paid no attention to them. Then I sat up and rubbed the sleep from my eyes. The voices were English. They belonged to a man and a woman and they were raised in anger. Clearly, those high-pitched, educated, carrying English voices came to me through the still air.

"I tell you", the man was saying, "the infernal thing won't start. I pressed the starter and all that happened was that it clicked at me. When I see Henson again I shall have something to say to him. He was supposed to have serviced the car for us. It's absolutely outrageous."

"Henson, dear," the woman's cool voice came, "is at a conservative estimate, seven hundred miles away. It's not much use cursing him. Can't we push it or something?"

"Push? We happen to have stopped at the bottom of the only upward slope in this stretch of road. The suggestion that we should push two tons of expensive machinery up an incline in gear in this heat is, to say the least of it, scarcely practical. In fact, of all the asinine suggestions you have made since this trip began I award that one the prize."

"I was not suggesting that *I* should push. If only you knew a little more about what went on under the bonnet, Hugo. . . ."

"I suppose you are now regretting that you did not marry a mechanic?"

"I'm not denying that one would be singularly useful at the moment."

"You were well aware, I think, that I was not what is commonly called 'good with one's hands'."

"It depends what you mean by that, doesn't it? I wonder what Carlotta thinks about your ability with your hands?"

"Let's leave Carlotta out of this. I certainly shan't give my cars to Henson again. I'll have a few words to say to him when I get home———"

"While you are doing that perhaps I can take time out with Carlotta. In the meantime neither of them is likely to help us very much."

"Perhaps we could get some peasants to push the thing."

"In this wilderness? There's nothing for it, Hugo, you'll have to walk for help."

Behind a tree, ten yards back from the road, I could see them both quite clearly. He was beside the car, a tall, thin and angular man with sharp features and elegant, long-fingered hands. The car was a drop-head coupé of a very expensive make. The woman was sitting in the passenger's seat. She had a long, rather horse-featured face and masses of magnificent dark hair. In a way she was rather striking-looking.

They wrangled on for a bit and finally she persuaded him that he would be likely to find some help on the main road that ran through the valley below. With very bad grace he set off and disappeared round a corner some fifty yards away. I gave him a few minutes and then I walked out of the trees.

She had lit a cigarette and was smoking it and reading a novel. I leant on the door. She had not heard me come up. When I spoke she jumped. "*Bonjour, Madame,*" I said. "*Puis-je vous aider?*"

Her lips parted. She looked anxiously down the road as if hoping that her husband would reappear. A big leather handbag lay beside her on the seat. She picked it up and put it on her lap. For an instant she looked terrified. You couldn't blame her. It was lonely up here and, dirty and unshaven, I must have presented a pretty wild appearance. Then she took hold of herself. I saw this happening and I admired her for it.

"I'm afraid I don't speak French," she said quite calmly. "Do you speak English?"

"Yes," I said. "What is wrong?"

For answer she leant forward and pressed the self-starter. A metallic click answered her and no more. "That's what is wrong," she said. "Can you do anything about it?" She was quite self-possessed now.

"I think so."

I got her to show me the tools and to open the bonnet. It took me at the most two minutes to tighten the loose battery connection, but I fiddled about a bit with my head in the engine and while I fiddled I thought. Obviously here was a heaven-sent opportunity of getting quickly to the coast. But how was I best to use it and how was I to get these people out of my way when I got there?

I straightened up and went back to the car. "Try her now," I said.

She stretched out her hand, switched on the ignition and pressed the starter. The engine gave an apologetic cough and then slid into the smooth purr of six luxurious, upper-crust cylinders.

She gave me a straight stare, frankly appraising me. I was reminded that the *l'oeil de dérober* is not confined to men. The fact that I spoke English had reassured her. She was not in the least frightened now. Opening her handbag she took out a flat, gold cigarette-case and handed it to me. Then she snapped on a jewelled lighter. Our fingers met as I steadied the flame to my cigarette.

The smoke on my empty stomach made my head spin for a second. I put my hand on the edge of the door to steady myself. When my vision cleared I found her gazing at me again with that cool, appraising stare. "You look a bit in need of running repairs yourself," she said.

I rubbed my chin with the back of my hand. Then I glanced at myself in the driving mirror. "I could do with a wash and a brush-up," I said. "Who did you think I was—Dominici?"

She stretched a long, shapely arm into the back of the car and handed me a small, rectangular pigskin case. Inside, when I unzipped it, was an electric razor.

"Perhaps that would help," she said. "Give me the flex." She took it and plugged it into a point in the fascia.

I got into the car and shaved in the driving mirror. Then I unplugged the razor, wrapped up the flex and put the whole issue back in the case. "Thanks," I said, "I feel a lot better now."

"That cigarette hit you, didn't it? Could you do with something to eat?"

"You're very observant."

"I was in the Wrens in the war. I've seen cigarettes hit empty stomachs before. There is a lunch-basket behind. Help yourself."

I got it out. There was everything—coffee and a bottle of wine, rolls and butter, cold chicken and sliced ham, a Camembert. I fell on it.

She sipped a glass of the wine while I ate. When I had finished I packed the basket again and put it back on the seat. I got in and sat behind the wheel. "I want to go to Lavandou," I said. "Where are you bound for?"

"Lavandou will do. Now that you are cleaned and fed, how did you come suddenly out of the sky to play the St. Bernard?"

"I was sleeping in the woods."

"Why?"

I turned and looked at her. Boldly her eyes met mine and stared back.

"If I told you, you wouldn't believe it."

She shrugged her shoulders. "You came. You fixed it. Thanks. I've no right to know more."

Our eyes seemed locked together. Hers were large and lustrous. At the back of them was some sort of mute appeal. We were very near to each other. Her thigh was hard against mine. Suddenly, in unison, our breaths started coming faster. Almost of its own volition my arm went along the back of the seat behind and around her shoulders.

"It might be better with the top up," she said. Her hand went out and flicked a switch on the fascia. With a sigh the hood behind us unfolded and began to rise. It slid across and above us, shutting out the sun. Inside now it was warm and dark.

She almost threw herself against me and her full moist mouth fastened itself on to mine. Here was a complication I had not envisaged.

Later she lay back looking at me. "It's so strange," she said. "Your coming like a faun out of the woods just when Hugo and I were washed up. He keeps a mistress, Hugo does. At least I think she's his mistress but they live on such a high astral plane, these people, that you never can be sure if anything is ever consummated. We thought we might be able to patch it up. That's why we came abroad. But the trip has been a disaster. He's wired her to come out. He's meeting her in Hyères. He doesn't know I saw the wire. Hugo can never quite get away with anything. His uselessness with the car was the last straw. I suddenly felt I wanted someone like I used to know—someone hard and competent. Then you walked in."

Maybe I was hard and competent. Maybe it was because up to now I had always been lurking under Rupert's shade that I had never guessed it. Maybe someone who had not known me as a mere sounding-board for Rupert would think that. After all I had got out from Stalag X2, though I had never quite been able to believe that it was I who had done it.

"It's these hills," I said. "It's the heat and the height together. They do something to you."

'Who are you? No, don't tell me. I don't want to know."

"I have to get to Lavandou," I said. "Can I drive your car?"

"Yes."

The engine started again without hesitation. I put her into gear and we slid off.

She reached out her hand to let the top down. I caught her fingers as they touched the switch. "No," I said. "No. Not yet. Not till I have gone."

She looked at me with fright dawning again in her eyes. "I'm not a criminal," I said. "There will be no complications for you about this trip. The people who are looking for me are a very private organization and they like to keep it that way."

Two miles down we passed her husband with a swish and a scurry. In the rear mirror I had a glimpse of his startled face before we were round the next curve.

"You can come back to him," I said.

"Yes. To drive him to Hyères."

We went on in silence. She was a lovely car. She held the road like a leech. I threw her round the curves enjoying every moment of it. This was better than foot-slogging on or possibly thumbing a ride on a lorry.

When we came to the main road through the foothills I turned to the right instead of climbing the Col to Bormes. Here I drove the willing engine through the gears and watched the needle swing round the big black dial of the speedometer. The engine, unprotesting, took it all in its stride, and seemed indeed to be willing me to ask of it more and more. In no time at all we were at the road junction where the way to the Corniche de Maures begins. I turned left across the traffic and dropped down into Lavandou.

My intention was to take a bus to Saint-Tropez and from there to approach Sainte-Marguerite by boat. That, I thought, was a sufficiently indirect approach. I drove down the grandiloquently named "Avenue des Commandos d'Afrique", turned to the left and parked in front of the Grand Hotel. I got out of the car and shut the door. I was in the act of turning to speak to my companion when I happened to glance across at the Goéland.

Sitting at one of the front tables chatting to the good-looking waiter were Rupert and Jacquie.

A step backwards took me into the cover of a Buick

parked alongside. By bending down I could look out through its rear window. As I watched, Rupert finished his Pastis and paid his bill.

They both got up and commenced to walk along the front towards me. I turned my back and pretended to be doing something with my shoe. They went on past the Grand Hotel and Le Circle. I had no trouble following their movements. His gait would mark him out anywhere as indeed would her honey-coloured hair and the short white dress she wore which set off the lines of her lovely body. He was wearing shorts, a loose shirt and the wide-strapped sandals of the coast. She had an arm through his and they laughed as they walked.

There was a bus drawn up by the ticket office for the boats to the Islands. Jacquie went into the *Syndicat d'Initiative* while Rupert sauntered on towards the bus. He glanced inside it and then his gaze ran over the people who were standing about. Jacquie left the *Syndicat d'Initative* and joined him. They walked over to the sea wall and sat down. Rupert took out a packet of cigarettes and lit one. They gave the air of people preparing for a long wait.

My entry into enemy territory by bus was effectively stopped.

I got into the car again. I didn't look at her. I stared out through the windscreen at the sun on the sea and the islands sleeping in the haze.

"I hate doing this," I said. "But I want to borrow your car again. Can I have it?"

"Yes."

"I've got to get to Saint-Tropez. I don't think anyone can have located me yet. But they might have done. If so they'll try to stop me. You had better wait here. I'll park the car on the port and put the ignition key in the glove box. You can pick the car up later. It's the best I can do. And—thanks."

"Somehow I don't think they'll stop you. I'm coming too."

"You may get hurt."

"I'll chance it."

I knew that she meant it. I thought, too, that she would be cool and dependable if it came to trouble. Her hands were broad, not unshapely, and very capable. I wondered where she had got the wet husband from and why she had married him.

My hand went out to start the car when I remembered the condition I was in. My shorts were torn and dirty, my coat and my shirt rumpled and stained. Even amongst the oddities at Saint-Tropez my present clothes would bring attention on to me. I could do with another pair of smoked glasses, too. I had long since lost those I had bought in Nice.

"I'd better get out of these clothes," I said. "Will you do some shopping for me?"

"Yes, if you tell me what you want."

"Dark glasses, jeans, a shirt, a light coat."

"That's a startling hair-cut. What about a straw hat as well?"

I grinned. "I don't usually affect this," I said. "True-fit and Hill will have six fits when I go back to them. You'll want money. This ought to cover it." I handed her a roll of 1,000-franc notes.

In twenty minutes she was back. From the car I saw her come round the corner by the Grand Hotel. She waited a second to let the traffic go by, and then crossed the road. She was tall, taller than I had thought seeing her only in the car, and she held herself well. Under her light clothes I could see the firm, strong outlines of her body. She had a brown paper parcel under her arm, her other hand carried a straw hat.

I took the hat and the glasses and put them on. "One more thing before we leave," I said. "A man and a girl were watching the bus stop. I want to know if they are still there. You can't mistake them. He is wearing a blue overshirt and white shorts. She has honey-coloured hair and looks like a million dollars."

She got out of the car without a word and walked towards the port. In a minute or two she was back. "They are still there," she said. She opened her cigarette-case and took one out. "She does look like a million dollars," she said.

I backed the car away from the park and turned into the town. I swung her round the corner between the post office and the newspaper shop and headed for the Corniche. She sat silently beside me, smoking.

"Is she why you are here?" she asked suddenly.

"No, or partly, perhaps."

"Love trouble," she said. "Everyone has love trouble. Though she looks as if she might be worth it."

"She isn't. Worth is a word which doesn't come into her vocabulary."

Telling her to keep an eye on the rear window in case we were picked up and tailed I laid the big car along. Saint-Clair, Cavalière, Aiguebelle, all the little villages with the lovely names, fled by.

We came to the vineyards of La Croix Valmer without incident. When we were amongst the firs I pulled in and stopped. Taking the parcel out of the back I left the car and went into the trees.

She was capable, all right. The jeans fitted me. So did the shirt and the jacket. Or at least the jacket fitted me as well as could be expected. The Luger made the hell of a bulge in the pocket but that couldn't be helped, either. The touch of clean clothes made me feel a lot better. Rolling the others into a ball I shoved them into a space between the roots of a tree.

When I came to the edge of the trees I saw a black *traction avant* drawn up behind her car. Two men in dark suits and felt hats were standing beside it, one at each door. I dodged back into cover and took out the Luger. I saw her hand come out of the front of the car and give something to one of the men. He stepped back, examined it, and then handed it back to her. He smiled, saluted and beckoned his companion. They got into the *traction avant* and drove off. Through the screen of trees I watched them go. For another ten minutes I waited there to see if they would return. They didn't. I stepped into the road and crossed to the car.

She was sitting in the driver's seat, smoking. Again she gave me that cool, appraising stare. "You can wear jeans," she said. "I wondered. Some men can't."

I jerked my head at the road. "What did they want?"

She did not take her eyes from me. "They were police officers. They were looking for an escaped criminal. An Englishman. About five feet ten inches. Speaks French fluently. Fair complexion. Brown hair. Dangerous. Is believed to be armed and may be violent. They warned me against him. They checked my papers."

"And you?"

"I told them I was much too discreet to stop on the road for strange men. They were most gallant."

"I'm sure. They were not police officers."

"I think I'd better drive. I got behind the wheel as they drove up. It would have looked unconvincing otherwise."

"You take to this quickly. I'm getting deeper and deeper into your debt."

"Forget it. It's been worth it to meet a man again."

"It's been worth it for one man to meet you."

She turned to me quickly. Her eyes suddenly filmed with tears. "Thank you for that," she said.

She drove competently and without fuss. The big car went on along without the snatch and start of so many women drivers. I told her to turn to the right at Croix-Valmer and we took the road to Ramatuelle.

"It's only a hunch," I said. "I don't think they are expecting me to go to Saint-Tropez at all. They think I'll go direct to a village called Sainte-Marguerite. They'll cover the main roads and the hills. We should be through the worst of it now."

"Let's have the top down, then."

I snapped up the switch and the hood subsided silently into the back. The sun and the sea were with us again. We did not speak as we went slowly along the narrow road. Now I had time to look at her properly There was no doubt she was striking-looking. She had smooth clear skin which the sun had tanned, large eyes and a firm strong mouth.

As we dropped down the hill below Ramatuelle I glanced at my watch. It was much earlier than I had thought. Although we had covered a considerable amount of ground since the morning we had not spent much time in doing it. I could not hope to try to cross the bay before nightfall and it was no part of my plan to spend the afternoon swanning about Saint-Tropez waiting to be shot at.

As if divining my thoughts she said: "How soon do you want to be there?"

"Not as early as this. I'll have to find somewhere to lie up. Drop me outside the town."

"No. We could bathe at Pampelonne."

"That's an idea. We would be lost there."

"Out of this world." She spun the wheel and we dropped down the long steep hill that leads between the fir trees to the sea.

There were only one or two cars parked at the end of the road where it runs on to the sands. She drew up beside them and went to the boot. Opening it she took out a beach bag. "Hugo's trunks are here if you can bear to wear them," she said.

"We'll take the picnic basket, too," I said. "I left a lot this morning and it's being borne in on me that we haven't had any lunch."

We walked far out across the sands and put down our burdens by the sea. Beyond the lighthouse two yachts chased each other, the triangles of their sails cutting across the blue of the sky. Except for a few black dots a mile away we were alone on the immense sweep of golden sand.

I kicked off the jeans and pulled on Hugo's trunks. Bending down I took the Luger from my jacket pocket. Sand and Lugers don't mix and I might have to use it tonight. I opened the lunch basket and laid it on the zinc lining.

She was standing beside me when I stood up. She was all but naked and she looked magnificent. Together we walked to the sea. The shelf there is very steep. In two steps we were swimming. She swam well, with strong, unhurried strokes. We went far out. Then we turned and lay on the buoyant surface of the water. One of the yachts came slanting down on us, changed

course and went away. The sun blazed. Below were
depths of blue and green; behind was the crescent of
golden sand. It was still, timeless. How long we stayed
there I do not know. Then, suddenly, she turned and
swam for the shore.

When I came in she was kneeling, shaking the glisten-
ing drops of water from her hair. Stretching full length
on the warm, gritty sand I let the sun sink into me and
dry the water from my body. She lay beside me and
she was so close to me I could feel the soft rise and fall
of her breathing. Drowsing in the heat, lazily, I ran
my hand along her arm. She gave a little gasp, smiled
and opened her eyes.

"I was sleeping," she said. "I dreamt I saw you—oh,
well, dreams. Dreams are for children. . . ." She sat
up and pulled the lunch basket towards her. Snapping
down the catches she opened it.

"Oh," she said. "Oh."

The Luger lay there. With its worn grip and the
rubs of use on its barrel and mechanism, it looked
sinister and menacing.

"It's part of something I have to do," I said quietly.

"Tonight?"

"I'm not sure but, yes, I think tonight."

She stared at the gun as if it were something evil, as
if a snake were among the food. "I said it didn't matter
who or what you were," she said. "But somehow, this
afternoon, this whole day, it's been for once right, it's
been so good——"

"I'm not a criminal," I said again, answering her unspoken question. "What I am going to do tonight is to find the end of an old, old story."

"With a gun?"

"Guns are not much, but sometimes you have to use them. When you do it's well to know how to use them right." Rupert, I thought, Rupert knew how to use a gun. It was he who had taught me to like a Luger. Come to think of it, it was he who had got me my Luger in the war.

She picked it up, not gingerly, but in a firm, sensible grip. "I don't think you'll use it wrong," she said, handing it to me and then, suddenly, her lips were on mine again.

It was evening when we came over the hill into Saint-Tropez. She slowed as we came through the Place Carnot.

"Do you want to get out here?" she asked.

"No," I said. "To hell with them. Go down to the port. We'll have a drink."

"I'd like that."

We went to Tante Marthe's. She asked for a dry martini. Tante Marthe's "drys" are second only to Herbert's. I ordered two. We sat sipping them and watching the people go by. When she had finished I asked her if she would have another. She shook her head. Her cigarette-case and the jewelled lighter were on the table in front of her. She picked up the case and put it in her bag. Then she stood up. She put out a finger and touched the lighter. "Keep that," she said quickly, abruptly. "It's for luck." Then she turned and walked away, down the port to the car. I saw her bend over the wheel, starting the car. She did not look back. The car swung into the traffic, was waved on by an *agent*, went steadily down the port and was gone.

I sat on. Tante Marthe brought me another martini. I picked up the little lighter and looked at it. I lit a cigarette with it and put it into my pocket. I don't know why but I suddenly felt more sure of myself, as if all the questions I had wondered about were going to be answered, as if my life were on rails at last.

I stood up and edged into the passing crowd, looking about me as I did so. Then I caught my breath. Two restaurants away Alakov was sitting, a *café noir* with a great blob of cream on it in front of him; beside him was the man in the check coat and the béret. I turned and walked away from Tante Marthe's, towards the old port.

A collection of people had gathered where the jetty runs out. They were watching the yachts and chatting and generally doing nothing in an elegant fashion. Mingling with them I allowed them to hide me. Then I looked back towards Alakov again. As I watched a *traction avant* drew to a standstill amongst the parked cars. Two men in suits and felt hats got out and walked over to Alakov's table. They stood in front of him and, when he nodded, sat down.

A few minutes later a big motor-boat came through

the harbour entrance. It made for a space between two yachts quite close to where I was standing. A man in white shorts and a loose shirt was at the wheel. As the boat approached the edge of the port he shut off the engine and sprang on to the forepeak. I could see him quite clearly. It was Rupert.

Calling to one of the bystanders he threw him a rope. Then he jumped down again and the engine went astern. The big boat came, very gently, up to the port.

The rope was made secure round a bollard. Rupert swung lightly ashore. He said to the man who was helping him that he would be back in a few minutes. Then he sauntered off down the port. I saw him join the group round Alakov's table. Without any ceremony he pulled out a chair and sat down, snapping his fingers at a waitress. Alakov was having an O group.

I waited. Presently Rupert got up from the table and began to walk back towards the boat. He was alone.

The crowd was still chatting and laughing and just plain idling all around me. I was anonymous and unseen. I walked to the edge of the port where the big motor-boat lay alongside. Nobody bothered about me. Three quick steps took me over the counter, down to the cockpit and into the cabin.

There were the usual bunks along each side with cushions on them, the usual polished mahogany and brass, the usual faint smell of paraffin, furniture polish and salt water. I wedged myself into the corner of one of the bunks, out of sight of the portholes. Hardly had

177

I done so than a figure darkened the doorway and Rupert came in. He stood for a moment, blinking, letting his eyes accustom themselves to the gloom after the sunlight outside.

At first he didn't see me. I lifted the Luger and pointed it at him.

"Sit down, Rupert," I said.

I did not take him at a disadvantage. I might have guessed that, of course. Coolly he looked across the cabin.

"You again," he said. Then he laughed. "If you only knew the trouble you've caused," he went on. "There is practically an armoured division looking for you. Besides, Alakov doesn't like his best Bentley's being reduced to scrap. I must say I never thought it of you."

"You'd be even more surprised if you knew how I got through the screen," I said. Somehow I felt more confident and capable of dealing with him now. My fingers touched the lighter in my pocket. She, at any rate, thought I was hard and competent.

"You haven't come here to appeal to my better nature, I hope," he said. "You ought to know by now that I haven't got any."

"Not much, I agree," I said, and for once I thought I had flicked him. "Listen, Rupert, there is something you can tell me now—it was Jacquie got you into this, wasn't it?"

It was the first time in all our acquaintance that I had seen him at a loss. He hesitated and his eyes strayed away from mine. Then he appeared to make up his mind. "Since you've guessed so much I may as well tell you," he said. "Yes, it was."

I knew then that I had been right all along, that my very first guess in the George V had gone to the heart of the matter. Jacquie had brought him here. It was the remnants of my love for her which had led me to shy away from the truth, which had led me to lose my temper with Rupert and to accept his airy lies when I had met him in Les Cascades. Had I not been such a fool I might have smashed the whole thing there and then. But strong emotions nurtured when young on love and war, die hard.

"By all that's merciful, Rupert! You of all people. Why did you do it?"

'It's like cheating at cards, isn't it, only worse? Well, Sir William Gordon-Cumming, Bart., of the Scots Fusilier Guards, cheated at baccarat in the presence of the heir to the throne—didn't he?"

"A jury said so."

"Don't be so damn smug, then. How do you know how you are going to behave when the heat is turned on? Take my cap and try it for size. Look at me and say, 'There but for the grace of God, go I.' "

"What the hell do you mean?"

"Jacquie is a Russian—pure-bred Russian for ten generations. She is an offspring of one of the few aristocratic families who pitched in with the Revolution and got away with it. She has been indoctrinated from birth

179

and by the Lord Harry she believes what she has been told. She says that she is French and she can prove it, too, but that is just another cover story. Shortly before the war she was put into England as a Soviet agent. As everyone now knows our methods of screening are puerile in the extreme. With her knowledge of languages and general ability she easily got the job in the ministry which she had when she took up with you. She hooked you, my lad, and you were being groomed for the high jump when I came along. I was always a sucker for a good-looking woman and doing you dirt didn't matter. You were so damned slow off the mark you deserved it, anyway."

"I've got a gun in my hand, Rupert."

If he heard me he made no sign. He went on, talking almost to himself. "It was cleverly done. I was, as usual, up to the neck with the books. She said she had a friend who ran a credit business who would be glad to open an account with me. I walked right in. Damn nice chap he was. Never pressed for payment—no awkward questions on settling day. Nothing at all until I was so deep in I couldn't get out. Then they made suggestions. It was little enough at first, just a hint about new weapons, a word about what was going on. Later they began to get more demanding. It surely didn't matter, they said. They were our allies, weren't they? It wasn't like giving information to the Germans. After all they were winning the war for us—all too easy for a chap whose conscience never troubled him too much. Then you started to find out things. I never meant to kill you. I just wanted you out of the way. But even without you things got too hot. We were sent to do a job in occupied France; Jacquie had by this time got herself into one of those cloak-and-dagger shows. Half the Maquis were Communists, as you know. We just disappeared."

"And afterwards?"

"They kept me here in luxury hoping that I'd be some use to them. Then they arranged my bogus death because, I think, awkward inquiries were being made from England. I was told to change my name and lie low. I'm watched wherever I go. Even this boat has only enough petrol to make the trip across and back, so don't get any idea of making a break in it. Some fellow from the Foreign Office, now in Moscow, wrote the book by the way—from the posthumous papers of Rupert Rawle."

"And now?"

"And now perhaps the sands are running out for me. Who knows?"

"They are. I know, or I think I know. Listen, Rupert——"

Suddenly above us was the sound of voices. I could distinctly make out Alakov's deep rasp. I looked up. Rupert was grinning at me his old derisive grin.

"You've been uncommonly foolhardy coming here to hear my testament, young Richard," he said. "Putting your head into the lion's mouth, eh?"

There was a door to a forward cabin beside me. I

181

reached over with my left hand and opened it. "I once read of a chap who did just that at a circus," I said. "He said his chief impression was the hell of a stink. At the moment I think I feel exactly the same." Then I was in the cabin with my foot against the door and my eye to the crack I had left between it and the lintel.

Ten

MOMENT OF TRUTH

They came into the cabin and sat down. Just Alakov and the tough were there. The two others had presumably gone off in the *traction avant*. At a nod from Alakov Rupert went out and started the engine. I heard the thresh and thump of the screw and we began to leave the quay. Then she turned. In a minute or two we were out into the gulf of Saint-Tropez. The waves slapped against the bows as the big boat gathered speed.

Rupert was at the wheel. The others sat without speaking on opposite sides of the saloon. Alakov had taken down a book of Navigational Instructions from a rack above his head and was glancing at it. The tough was smoking a cigarette. Rupert had made no move to give me away. Probably, even if he were going to, he would not choose this time to do it. If he did, were I to start shooting first, I had a very good chance of killing the three of them before they got me. We were only three yards from each other. I prayed that the tension I felt would not communicate itself to them, that they would not sense my presence.

The tough ground out his cigarette in a brass ashtray. He stood up and looked out of the door of the cabin. Then he turned and started to prowl around. He came nearer to where I was. I held my breath. This is it, I thought, he's coming in. The Luger was centred on the middle of his great belly. He was within a foot of me when the skirts of his coat hit the ashtray and knocked it off the table. It fell to the deck with a clatter. Alakov looked up. "Sit down," he said, and went back to his book. The big man turned and sat heavily down on one of the bunks. He put his hands on his knees and closed his eyes. I could hear his heavy breathing. The boat ran on. The minutes dragged by.

After an eternity I heard the note of the engine change. Glancing out of a porthole I saw the grey walls of a jetty going by. We were in the little harbour of Sainte-Marguerite. Rupert cut the engine and we came gently alongside. Alakov put the book back in the rack. Without moving he called Rupert into the cabin.

"I am expecting Miss Leroux at eight o'clock to-night," he said. "She is joining me for a drink. I shall not detain her long. She will be back with you for dinner. Stackman will go with you."

I saw Rupert nod and the three of them left the cabin.

Now was the crucial time. Would he tell them of my presence as soon as they stepped ashore? Gun in hand I went into the main cabin. All was still. The portholes here showed above the edge of the port. I looked out. Dusk was falling. I could see the three of them walking away. The pale blue Cadillac was parked at the edge of the port. They got into it and were driven off.

I didn't waste any time. Leaving the boat I made the best of my way into the town.

Eight o'clock at Les Cigales—that was the deadline. Somehow or other I had to be there too, and I hadn't much time. My most immediate need was a car. I would have preferred to walk for I did not know what sort of road blocks they would have established round the house, but time would not let me.

There were usually two taxis parked in the Place, underneath a gaudy yellow board with a chart of tours to Cannes and the Gorges du Loup drawn on it. The board was there but both the taxis were gone. A by-stander told me they had been hired for the afternoon. He added that they would probably be back "any minute". A Provençal's assessment of "any minute" is much the same as an Irishman's. It might mean an hour and it might mean five hours—or two minutes. Remembering that the garage where I got my petrol sometimes hired cars I made for it.

The proprietor eyed me suspiciously when I said I wanted to hire a car for the night. He was not a very accommodating chap at the best of times. Now he kept growling all sorts of objections and darting sidelong glances at me. It was quite dark and he wore spectacles so I supposed he couldn't see very well. My nerves were getting edgy. Time was racing by and I wasn't just going to pay a social call. How long it was going to take me to penetrate the defences of Les Cigales I didn't know, but it certainly wasn't going to be a matter of strolling up the drive and being admitted by the butler. I took out two notes and waved them at him.

He looked at them and then at me. He came a bit nearer and peered into my face. Then, telling me to wait a minute, he shuffled off into the black depths of the garage.

I sat down on a pile of old tyres and lit a cigarette. Cars went by on the road outside. Consumed with impatience, I drew on the cigarette and cursed the old fool. Suddenly it occurred to me that he was taking a long time about whatever he was doing. Surely all this delay wasn't necessary merely to fill up a car? Once again all sorts of warning bells went off in my mind.

I stood up and looked about me. At the very back of the garage was a faint glow of light and I thought I could make out the old man's figure bending over something. Throwing my cigarette into the road I groped my way through the darkness, barking my shins on odd pieces of metal. Once I narrowly missed falling into an inspection pit, but the light led me on.

It came from a wood and glass partition built out from one wall to form an office. Inside was the old man. He was bending over a telephone. I put my ear to the partition.

"*La Poste?*" I heard him saying. "M. Dubois? The

man with the *quatre chevaux*. The one about whom you were inquiring. The one which was smashed near Le Revest. He is here now. I am certain it is the same. I will keep him until you come."

"That you won't," I said to myself, and legged it out of the place.

Now I had the ruddy police as well as everybody else after me. There was nothing for it but to look for the taxis in the Place again. I was afraid to run lest I draw attention to myself. As quickly as I could I walked down the road and turned to the left by the post office.

One of the taxis had come in. A car went through the Place, lights flaring, horn blazing. That, I supposed, was M. Dubois out for the kill.

A horde of tourists were getting out of the taxi and were taking an unconscionable time about it. More children than I would have believed possible came out of the back. Then paterfamilias started to have a row with the driver about the bill. The row developed and became noisy. Heads began to turn. I backed away. As I did so one of the taximan's friends joined in. Then mama, in a bombazine dress, came up as reinforcement to her husband. Two of the children started to scream. Bystanders began to gather and to take sides. Altogether, it was no place for me.

Beyond the plane trees, near an *alimentation*, I saw a man leaning on an ancient Renault watching the fracas with a grin on his face. Then he shrugged his

187

shoulders and got into the car. The Renault was pointing in the direction of Le Muy. I took a chance and walked up to him.

"If you are going towards Le Muy could you give me a lift?" I asked.

"Sure thing, Major," he answered in accents of the purest Brooklyn. "Hop in."

We made our way out of the village and started to climb for the hills. No one followed us. For the moment, anyway, M. Dubois must have been busy, like his illustrious compatriots Poirot and Hanaud, looking for clues. Nor were we interfered with on the road. There were no road blocks, no plug-uglies hanging about. The guards of the villa must, I thought, all be inside the grounds. That there were guards I was certain. This was the culmination of Alakov's plans. He would leave nothing to chance. This was the pay-off.

It transpired that my driver had served with the Americans during the war and we chatted about this and that as we drove along. Some distance past the entrance to Les Cigales I asked him to let me down. From the side of the road I stood and watched his red tail light fade away into the distance.

When the car had disappeared I took out the Luger and checked the action. There was a round in the chamber. I made sure that the safety was on and then shoved the gun into the waistband of my jeans.

It was dark in the woods and I had to take it slowly. I didn't know how far the screen of guards would stretch. For all I knew it might only be the house itself which was guarded, but I could not afford to make any mistakes.

I was flat on my stomach and, I reckoned, about fifty yards from the drive when I met the first of them. He was making a noise like a bull elephant going through underbrush. One of his boots came down a foot from my face as he lumbered past. It was easily seen that Rupert had had no hand in his training. I let him get some distance away and began to crawl forward.

A little farther on I found the second thing I was looking for. It was about a foot from the ground and stretched tight. It was either a trip or an alarm wire or, more probably, both. In any event I treated it with respect and took care not to touch it. Then I was at the edge of the drive.

The guard on the drive was plain to be seen. He was walking up and down with almost military precision. He had a sawn-off shotgun on the crook of his arm. He didn't seem too happy about his job for he kept turning his head from side to side and twisted jumpily about to peer in the direction of the slightest noise. I made a guess that these toughs would be more at home in city streets with houses about them than out here in the hills.

I slipped across the drive when he was at the other end of his beat. Crouching under a cork oak I waited and watched, trying to locate the guards at this side. Nothing stirred. If there were any here they were either better trained or else took more care to conceal their presence than the ones I had passed.

I had removed my watch lest its luminous dial give me away, but I knew that it had taken time to get where I was. It must now at least be close on eight o'clock. But I dare not hurry. Any false move might ruin all that I had done, all that I had come for. I edged slowly forward towards the house.

Then, at last, I saw him. He was standing against a tree. He, too, had a gun across his arm. It was that which first drew my eyes to him. He was between me and the house. There was no question of avoiding him. I had to get him were I to live. And I had to do it in silence.

Foot by foot I got nearer to him. He didn't move. He was as still as the tree itself. I breathed slowly, evenly, silently, through my open mouth. Still his figure remained motionless. I wondered if he had seen me and was waiting for me. Even if he had not I must cover the five yards which now separated us without giving him time to move. My life lay in those five yards. Even if I got him and he had time to touch a trigger I was done for.

A car came up the drive. Its lights flashed through the trees. The purr of its engine came abreast of us. The guard moved. So did I.

I don't think I killed him. But I may have done. I couldn't take any chances. I slammed the Luger with all my strength into the back of his head. He never made a sound. I caught him as he slumped forward, and then got the gun before it hit the ground. It was a sawn-off shotgun with the safety off.

Opening the gun I took the shells out of it and pushed it away into the undergrowth. Then I strapped the man's hands with his belt and shoved his handkerchief into his mouth. Nobody else came along to investigate. Very carefully I moved towards the house.

A light sprang on in the room in front of me so suddenly that I was almost caught in the illuminated rectangle it threw on the grass. From where I crouched in the imperfect cover of a cactus I could see across this rectangle through the long french windows and into the room beyond. Two people had entered the room. They were Alakov and Jacquie. A bottle of champagne stood in an ice-bucket on the table. Beside it on a silver tray were two glasses.

Alakov crossed to the table. Under his arm he had a rectangular cardboard box. This he put on the table whilst he busied himself opening the champagne.

Jacquie looked radiant. By and large I had never seen her looking more beautiful.

Alakov poured the champagne. Then he turned to the box and opened it. From it he took a lady's handbag with a diamond clasp. He motioned her to come towards him.

I had to find out what they were saying. Where I crouched was out of earshot. Down the edge of the rectangle of light I made my way on my hands and knees. There was a tiny stone terrace beside the window. Here I was only a few feet from the interior of the room. I could hear everything they said. And I could see what Alakov was doing. His short, squat fingers moved over the stitching at the side of the bag. A small section came away and he took out a tiny, thin booklet. This he held up to her and laughed. "The code," he said, smiling. Then he lifted his glass. "To success."

"To success," Jacquie's voice echoed him and their glasses touched.

"All arrangements have been made," Alakov's voice ground on. "Tomorrow you will join Sir Hussey Higgins's yacht at Deauville. He is looking forward to meeting the beautiful Contessa di Valois whose husband died so horribly in a concentration camp in Poland. He sails for Southampton the following day. You will be met there. Nothing can go wrong." He filled the glasses again. "But listen carefully once more to these final instructions. It is essential that the revelation be made at just the right time. . . .

Outside the window I heard in detail the full part which Rupert's book and Rupert himself and Rupert's name was to play in the plot.

I turned, treading softly. The body of the guard lay where I had left it. It was damned ingenious, the whole scheme, I thought as I went. But had they made certain, I wondered, that Rupert would do as they wished? That was something I must find out from Rupert himself. Here was where he and I came to the final reckoning.

When I reached the road I started to run. I ran all the way to Les Cascades. I was panting and retching from the drag up the hill when I got there, and for a few seconds I leant against the end of the house recovering my breath.

Rupert was on the dining terrace. He had put down a glass of Pastis which he had evidently been drinking and was looking at the label of a bottle which he held in his hand. "Ste. Roseline," he said, as I came up. "A charming wine, I've always thought, though they tell me it doesn't travel. We'll have it for dinner, I think. Perhaps you'll stay?" His mocking glance was full on me.

"Rupert," I said. "The sands have run out. You leave for Moscow tomorrow. Do you know that? Do you know what you are going to have to do?"

He put the bottle down on the table. "Indeed, yes," he said. "I have known for a little time now although I'm afraid our friend Alakov is not aware of that. Every organization has a weak link and I took the precaution of finding that link here. Hence my information. This, dear boy, is what I've been fattened for over the years like a Strasbourg goose. An Anglo-American conference opens in Paris in two days' time in an atmosphere of doubt and mistrust. On the eve of its opening Moscow announces yet another defection to its cause. Major Rupert Rawle, the mystery man of M.I.5, has become converted to Communism. He has fled to Moscow and taken with him the secrets of the British Secret Service

—if any. It will be Douglas Hyde in reverse. Clever and well timed, don't you think? The announcement will not exactly lighten the tension between the two countries at this difficult period in their relationship. And it will be very difficult to show that I was not a man from M.I.5. You see, I was never quite disowned. I was in a cloak-and-dagger show when I disappeared. At home they've never been actually able to prove that I was working for the Soviet. Come to think of it I haven't much, anyway. Both sides thought I might come in useful sometime. When I was killed off it didn't suit anyone to make a scandal out of me. Although now I think those at home may be wishing that they had. But Robinson & Co., I've always believed, nourished the faint hope that I might come home to weep on their breasts and tell all.

"Well, they've been beaten to the gun, as usual. The Russians are using me now. I don't flatter myself by saying that they are playing their ace; they are playing a very useful knave, perhaps." He chuckled as he always did when he said something which amused him. "Yes," he went on, "it's going to be very hard to disown me when this hits the headlines. Everyone knows that a country abandons its agents once they step out of line and such disclaimers never carry conviction. The American papers two days hence should make interesting reading. And that isn't all. There is our little Jacquie. She has a part to play, too. . . ."

We both turned at the noise of a car being garaged

below us. Jacquie came up the steps and walked into the light.

"Ah, my dear," Rupert said, "I was just telling our friend the part you have to play in the great scheme—the apotheosis of Rupert Rawle. Tomorrow evening", he went on, turning to me again, "Jacquie will be in England travelling incognito with Sir Hussey Higgins, the well-known industrialist. The following day there will be handed in to the *Daily World* the key to the code in which certain passages in my book are written. A note will accompany it telling that admirable organ to get in touch with the publishers. The passages, when decoded, contain the reasons, in some detail, how and why a pillar of the Secret Service became disgusted with Western democracy, and they also reveal some interesting sidelights on recent American secret history. The book, as I told you, was written by a gentleman in Moscow, lately of the British Foreign Service in Washington. Those passages are dynamite. Do you know, I don't somehow think that the conference will be a great success."

"Why are you telling him this?" Jacquie said in icy tones. "Have you gone mad, Rupert? Don't you know that he has caused enough trouble? Get rid of him. He has gone too far now. I'm afraid, Rupert," and her voice was cold, expressionless, without compassion or feeling, "you will have to kill him."

"Unfortunately, my dear," Rupert's calm voice replied, "he has a gun in his belt and I have no doubt that he is ready to use it. That he is able to use it I also know because I taught him. He seems to have grown up quite a bit, recently, our little Richard. Perhaps we underrated him, my dear. Also, I hate to remind you that your employers never liked leaving firearms about where I was. There is very little, I fear, that I can do. Perhaps we'd all better have a glass of Ste-Roseline."

"Fool! I suppose you are afraid of him."

"There is something in having no self-respect, Richard, it renders one impervious to insult. Yes, I'm afraid of him."

There was a bump from the back quarters and then a crash.

"Stackman appears to be having even more trouble than usual cooking dinner," Rupert observed.

The door behind us was thrown open and Morel strode in. He carried the big army Colt in his right hand. "Get your hands up—all of you," he commanded. "And don't move. I'm quite prepared to shoot." He paused in the middle of the room, his eyes gleaming in triumph. "I have the whole plot now," he went on. "If you are looking for a needle in a haystack, it's best to use a very strong magnet which will draw it out. I left that gun with you deliberately, Graham. I knew that you could not resist coming back to your old friend and your lost love. You have been watched ever since you left the Abbaye Calumet, except for a few hours this afternoon. Where were you?"

"I was out of this world," I said.

"We had only to follow you to find what we wanted. The driver of the car who took you to Les Cascades was one of my men. I have heard everything Rawle said. I had to deal with one of your men, Rawle, before I came in."

"Morel's such a clever chap, isn't he?" I said.

Morel ignored this. "I'm taking you all in now," he said. "I have a car outside. Come, immediately. This is one Soviet *coup* which will not materialize. I have foiled it."

"I hate to interrupt this one man admiration society," Rupert said. "But, judging by the activity I see below, Alakov and his men are coming up after you and you may not get away quite as easily as you think."

From the terrace we could see Les Cigales. Lights were springing on all over the house. Car lights flashed from the garage at the back. They must have found the body I had left lying about. Jacquie gave a little laugh.

"Not quite clever enough, *mon ami*," she said to Morel.

"If you give me that gun, Morel," Rupert said quietly, "I'll hold them off for you, at least long enough for you to get the others away."

"You . . ." Morel said contemptuously. "You don't expect me to trust you, Rawle. . . ."

Rupert sighed. "Always my fate to be distrusted," he said softly. "Yet you might as well, you know. I've nothing to lose, this time. I'm not going through with this play-acting. It's a bit too much even for me.

197

Richard knows that, I think, dont you, Richard? They never quite bought me."

"I thought so when you let me go after I had traced you here," I said. "I knew it when you didn't give me away on the boat."

Jacquie looked over her shoulder. "They're in the road now," she said. "You're caught. You can't get away."

"So it seems you've nothing to lose either, Morel," Rupert said. "In any event I don't propose to adopt this ridiculous posture any longer."

It happened so quickly I couldn't follow it. With his left hand he knocked Jacquie out of the line of fire. In one motion his right hand jerked the Luger from my waist and fired it.

There was an answering boom from Morel's gun. The slug screeched past me and smashed, tinkling, into the bottles on the drink tray at our backs. Then Morel was holding a wrist from which a slow drop of blood began. His gun was on the floor at his feet.

"Not quite quick enough," Rupert said to him. "That's too much gun for you, Morel. Little men shouldn't play with big toys." Then he turned to Jacquie. "So it ends," he said gently. "You see, my dear, I loved you once. Oh, yes, I did. That's why I came away with you. Not for blackmail or promises of an easy life or for any other reason but just like any other fool, just for love. But it didn't last. It couldn't, could it? You are not a woman really. Your body is only an instrument of policy. I think Richard knows that now, too. Your mind—well, I don't know how the mind of a fanatic works, my dear, but at least it doesn't include human beings in its workings. They are only chessmen to be moved on a board. So not any more, not for years now, not any more. Unfortunately, like all the other fools who sold the pass for a woman, I found out too late."

Leaning against the wall she drew herself up. Again for an instant she looked radiant. "Nothing is quite as simple as we make it sound," she said. "Perhaps I loved you, too—once—Rupert. You will never know now."

"Richard, you're in charge. Get them out of here. There's a road to the right a hundred yards beyond the house. No one knows it; it's only a track really, but it will take you to Plan de la Tour. I'll deal with our friends below. I've been waiting for this for a long, long time."

"Rupert, wait. Come with us. . . ."

"No."

"Then I must stay, too."

He stepped forward, picked up Morel's gun and threw it over the terrace. "You can't stay now," he said. "Besides, I want to finish this myself, my own way, the way I've always done."

"Rupert——"

"It's no use, Richard. I thought this out long ago. Chance and you have put a gun into my hand. There is nothing else left for me. You know that, too, I think. Go now, Richard."

He was right; there was nothing else left for him. Nothing. The sands had run out. The glass was empty.

At the door I paused and looked at him. He was standing with the gun in his hand, staring out to sea. He turned and smiled the old mocking smile.

"*Le dernier cochon*," he said. "The ultimate four-letter man. Adieu, *mon vieux*."

I raised my hand in salute. "Good-bye, Rupert," I said. Then I pushed the door open and ran blindly out to the car.

We were ten yards down the road when I heard the firing begin.

Eleven

PUBLISHER'S REMAINDER

I swirled the brandy in the balloon glass, lifted it and drank. It occurred to me that I had been drinking rather a lot in the last few days. I felt no particular inclination to stop. The portraits on the walls stared down upon us. We had sat on after dinner and were almost alone in the long, shaded dining-room of the Garrick Club.

"Well, there it is," I said. "That is the story. I haven't got your typescript back, I'm afraid."

"They stopped the projected sabotaging of the conference."

"Oh, yes. There wasn't much they could do about it with Rupert dead, Jacquie in gaol and the code impounded. Morel managed the round-up of their agents very neatly. No fuss, no publicity. He has a hole in his hand, though. Every time he looks at it it may take some of the conceit out of him."

Robin Saunders leant his elbows on the table. "What about you?" he asked.

"I don't know. Have you ever felt that everything has gone sour on you? They were my friends, after all, and old ties are strong. Besides, no one is ever really black or really white, are they?"

"So the novelists say."

"Yes, well some of us have to find out these things for ourselves. From that very first time she came to me in Paris I guessed that Jacquie was at the root of it all as far as Rupert was concerned. Just how strongly she controlled him I don't think I knew until the very end. In her own way she may have been a little in love with him, too—once. I like to think so, anyway."

"You promised me a book, you know," Saunders said, quite gently for him. "You wouldn't like to write it now?"

"No," I said. "Not now."

"Maugham once said that writers have an immense advantage over everyone else in that they can write down an experience and get it out of their system."

"Perhaps, but I'm not a writer."

"We could knock it into shape for you."

"Leave it like that," I said. "Later, perhaps I will."

I took the little jewelled lighter out of my pocket and lit a cigarette. When I had finished I put it on the table beside the glass.

"That is a curiously feminine thing for you to have," Saunders said sharply, his eyes fastening on to it. "I've not seen you with it before. Has it anything to do with the story?"

I stared at it winking up at us from the polished table-top.

"I'm not sure," I said. "Maybe it has everything to do with the story. When I've thought it all out perhaps I'll write it for you."

I picked the lighter up and put it in my pocket. Then I finished the brandy.

THE PERENNIAL LIBRARY MYSTERY SERIES

Delano Ames

CORPSE DIPLOMATIQUE	P 637, $2.84
FOR OLD CRIME'S SAKE	P 629, $2.84
MURDER, MAESTRO, PLEASE	P 630, $2.84
SHE SHALL HAVE MURDER	P 638, $2.84

E. C. Bentley

TRENT'S LAST CASE	P 440, $2.50
TRENT'S OWN CASE	P 516, $2.25

Gavin Black

A DRAGON FOR CHRISTMAS	P 473, $1.95
THE EYES AROUND ME	P 485, $1.95
YOU WANT TO DIE, JOHNNY?	P 472, $1.95

Nicholas Blake

THE CORPSE IN THE SNOWMAN	P 427, $1.95
THE DREADFUL HOLLOW	P 493, $1.95
END OF CHAPTER	P 397, $1.95
HEAD OF A TRAVELER	P 398, $2.25
MINUTE FOR MURDER	P 419, $1.95
THE MORNING AFTER DEATH	P 520, $1.95
A PENKNIFE IN MY HEART	P 521, $2.25
THE PRIVATE WOUND	P 531, $2.25
A QUESTION OF PROOF	P 494, $1.95
THE SAD VARIETY	P 495, $2.25
THERE'S TROUBLE BREWING	P 569, $3.37
THOU SHELL OF DEATH	P 428, $1.95
THE WIDOW'S CRUISE	P 399, $2.25
THE WORM OF DEATH	P 400, $2.25

Julian Symons

THE BELTING INHERITANCE	P 468, $1.95
BLAND BEGINNING	P 469, $1.95
BOGUE'S FORTUNE	P 481, $1.95
THE BROKEN PENNY	P 480, $1.95
THE COLOR OF MURDER	P 461, $1.95

Dorothy Stockbridge Tillet
(John Stephen Strange)

THE MAN WHO KILLED FORTESCUE	P 536, $2.25

Simon Troy

THE ROAD TO RHUINE	P 583, $2.84
SWIFT TO ITS CLOSE	P 546, $2.40

Henry Wade

THE DUKE OF YORK'S STEPS	P 588, $2.84
A DYING FALL	P 543, $2.50
THE HANGING CAPTAIN	P 548, $2.50

Hillary Waugh

LAST SEEN WEARING . . .	P 552, $2.40
THE MISSING MAN	P 553, $2.40

Henry Kitchell Webster

WHO IS THE NEXT?	P 539, $2.25

Anna Mary Wells

MURDERER'S CHOICE	P 534, $2.50
A TALENT FOR MURDER	P 535, $2.25

Edward Young

THE FIFTH PASSENGER	P 544, $2.25

If you enjoyed this book you'll want to know about THE PERENNIAL LIBRARY MYSTERY SERIES

Buy them at your local bookstore or use this coupon for ordering:

Qty	P number	Price
_____	_____	_____
_____	_____	_____
_____	_____	_____
_____	_____	_____
_____	_____	_____
_____	_____	_____
_____	_____	_____
_____	_____	_____
_____	_____	_____
_____	_____	_____
_____	_____	_____
_____	_____	_____
_____	_____	_____
_____	_____	_____
_____	_____	_____
_____	_____	_____

	postage and handling charge	$1.00
	_____ book(s) @ $0.25	_____
	TOTAL	[ ]

Prices contained in this coupon are Harper & Row invoice prices only. They are subject to change without notice, and in no way reflect the prices at which these books may be sold by other suppliers.

HARPER & ROW, Mail Order Dept. #PMS, 10 East 53rd St., New York, N.Y. 10022.

Please send me the books I have checked above. I am enclosing $_____ which includes a postage and handling charge of $1.00 for the first book and 25¢ for each additional book. Send check or money order. No cash or C.O.D.s please

Name_____

Address_____

City_____ State_____ Zip_____

Please allow 4 weeks for delivery. USA only. This offer expires 10/31/84. Please add applicable sales tax.